Shanghai 2040

Shanghai 2040

Jean-Louis Roy

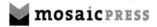

Library and Archives Canada Cataloguing in Publication

Title: Shanghai 2040 / Jean-Louis Roy.

Other titles: Shanghai 2040. English | Shanghai twenty forty | Shanghai two thousand forty

Names: Roy, Jean-Louis, 1941- author.

Description: Translation of: Shanghai 2040.

Identifiers: Canadiana (print) 20220250073 |
           Canadiana (ebook) 20220250081 |

ISBN 9781771616522 (softcover) | ISBN 9781771616539 (PDF) |
ISBN 9781771616546 (EPUB) | ISBN 9781771616553 (Kindle)

Classification: LCC PS8585.O8984 S5313 2022 | DDC C843/.54—dc23

Published by Mosaic Press, Oakville, Ontario, Canada, 2022.

MOSAIC PRESS, Publishers
www.Mosaic-Press.com

Copyright © Jean-Louis Roy 2022

MOSAIC PRESS
1252 Speers Road, Units 1 & 2, Oakville, Ontario, L6L 5N9
(905) 825-2130 • info@mosaic-press.com • www.mosaic-press.com

OTHER BOOKS BY JEAN-LOUIS ROY

Africa.com: Digital, Economic, Cultural Transformations
(Mosaic Press, 2021)
Mansa Musa I - Kankan Moussa: From Niani to Mecca
(Mosaic Press, 2019)
The Age of Diversity: The New Cultural Map
(Mosaic Press, 2016)
Ontario in Transition: Achievements and Challenges
(Mosaic Press, 2013)

"You have lived too long in New York, I told her. There exist other worlds and other dreams."

TABLE OF CONTENTS

CHAPTER I

THE FIRST DAY

BEIJING, NOVEMBER 2036

Wei Shu is world famous. Her code names are legion: she is "Lightening" in Washington, "The Feline" in Tokyo, "The Slum" in Delhi, "The Gentlewoman" in Berlin, "Mr. Fixated" in Moscow, "The Power Woman" in Abuja. In China, in the Asiatic countries and in the vast Chinese diaspora in Asia and the world, she is called "The Empress".

Wei Shu choreographed in minute detail all the sequences for her first day as President of the Popular Republic of China. *This day belongs to me*, she writes in her diary, *"as henceforth I belong to China and China, to the world.*

Once gum has bonded with shellac, who could ever succeed in separating them?

She has longed for this office and this power. By quoting for her close collaborators that excerpt from an ancient poem, she expresses her desire to impose, from this very first day, the image of a resolute boss at the helm of the foremost world power.

"Leader of the World," read the headlines of the *New York Times* under a superb full page color photo of Wei Shu. She liked the photo and its layout, a little less the text that she described as "too shifty, too hesitant." The world's social networks buzz with judgements, assessments and commentaries on this woman who is both elegant and discreet, bold yet cautious, restrained but capable of decisive strikes. She is called a "lioness" by the leaders of the Party and a "gazelle" in the government, "or the opposite," according to her *shifu*.

Some elevate her to the summit of intuition and strategic intelligence, others evoke her private life, her supposedly lascivious

1

liaisons in New York as well as in Berlin and Paris. Finally, her relationship with the man who is called her *shifu*, or mentor, is analyzed from every angle: the latter was supposedly a Saudi Arabian spy; the rival of the Moroccan king; an Egyptian gigolo; an Indian mercenary, and that was not all. This close friend of the President is unrestrainedly roasted. Cartoonists around the world have drawn up on him an impressive collection of "twisted images"; just like the Chinese, American, Russian, Israeli, Saudi secret services and other "reputation scroungers," their files varying according to the capitals and allegiances. With their laser-eyed drones, the paparazzi have taken photos of her, not all of which are impeccable. They all disappeared mysteriously, bought up by agents with persuasive chequebooks. Obviously, the Chinese social medias are the exception. And what an exception! There the leader of the foremost world power is literally canonised: "the star of diplomacy master classes"; an intelligence that goes beyond the best conceived algorithms"; "the negotiator of thousands of successes"; the internet surfers go beyond the threshold of privacy and celebrate the unique beauty of the "mother of the nation"; others exalt her very classic elegance, "the classic Chinese one," according to the sister of that dazzling sexagenarian. They also celebrate the "Daughter of the Party," who has never had any other family.

Her election was prepared well in advance, she confessed one day to the members of her personal cabinet while breaking out laughing, "from the time I took control of the Youth League, in 1997."

"For the first time, the *People's Daily* publishes my photo, placing me arbitrarily, indeed falsely, in the conservative wing of the Party. As a result, leader of the Youth League, I gain access to the Central Committee as one of the two thousand five hundred delegates. But I don't go unnoticed. I have a clientele, the young people, and in the thousands; a publication that was in the spotlight; a title, precious speaking time and the famous blue pass that authorizes me to attend all workshops.

"For the first time, I follow the deliberations that precede the choice of the two hundred members of the Central Committee, of the twenty-five members of its political bureau and of those belonging to its permanent committee. You know what is said of all the glossy speeches delivered in these contexts. They are like the clucking of frogs that devour serpents from within. I turned myself into a frog.

"The deliberations are followed by decisive phases, by negotiations that are very hard-driven, indeed virulent, supposedly semi-public, but, in truth, totally private. I was not entirely aware of that at the time. I would sometimes discover it at my expense during the seven quinquennial meetings of the Central Committee in which I have participated since. I have not missed even one of them in thirty-five years. I have known a few defeats, but above all a stream of little victories which, added together, tipped the scales."

China's hour of glory had returned after the century of every possible humiliation and every possible exploitation. The President set up two complementary markers: image control and message control.

The project manager of activities during the early days of the presidency is a faithful among the faithful. Successively principal administrator of programs involving the New Silk Road, then director of the Party's Central School, Che Se combines world networks and national networks, the management of the ambitions, demands and "rare whims of the boss," as the latter calls them, then on a daily basis follows up on "the health" of the internal as well as external political situation of the country. In other words, he watches over the daily life of the Party and the government. When a deputy asked him to define his function as Director of the President's personal cabinet, he replied: "I am in charge of the security of the world, of China and of the President, and in the order that suits you, the three being so interdependent."

A friend of the president since their childhood, he has belonged for the past fifteen years to the select club of her close counsellors. He was with her at the Ministry of Finance, then at the Chinese Mission at the United Nations in New York.

The President says to her close friends, "Che Se has four eyes, one for the Party and the three others as well! Let's be serious, one for the Party and its one hundred and twenty million members, another for the State and its one billion three hundred million citizens, a third for the Net and its billions of Chinese and other surfers, finally, one last one for my humble person."

As the Director of the personal cabinet called the civil cabinet of the President, Che Se coordinates the work of the teams that comprise more than four hundred specialists representing all that matters in the agendas of national and international politics. He also takes care of the presidential calendar, answers telephone calls from heads of state and foreign governments, from the prime minister and the most important ministers in the government, those as well from the President of the Central Bank, from the three principal heads of the National Revolutionary Army and from its sentinels "wherever there is oxygen," according to a Hong Kong clandestine satirical sheet.

Every morning and every evening, he meets with Wei Shu and relates to her everything that reinforces or threatens the Party and the government's strategic plan. Their discussions always end with the same phrase spoken by Wei Shu: "Any other issue or issues and situations not brought up that deserve my attention?"

As the Director of her cabinet, he belongs to her second family. One enters it with joy and one leaves it with fear. He is the one who knows everything, or almost everything, about the private life of his boss: her relationship with her *shifu*, her life as well with her next of kin, her father and father-in-law, her first husband, who is the father of her two children, her only sister, the cluster of uncles and aunts and their offspring, the "normal" friends, few but very present, consisting of a circle of painters and writers whom she likes and brings together once a year. There are "abnormal" friends, too, numerous and all bearing the insignia of the Party "whether they are believers or not."

To this list is added the house staff which is like another family: the private secretaries and information agents, the children's caregivers and tutors-counsellors, the major-domos, the chefs, their assistants and the servers, the florists and gardeners, the art collection curators, the chauffeurs, personal bodyguards and the others.

There are also the President's hairdressers, make-up artists and dressers in charge of her wardrobe. In their majority they are distant cousins from the ancestral village. When the President was an adolescent, she and they disguised themselves as ancient personages, with red makeup, and leaped together over the fire of the Spring Feast to rid themselves of bad influences. In the President's dwelling they use a dialect over which their boss has an almost complete mastery, but which is a real foreign language for the rest of the staff. They prepare the daily outfits for Madame to choose. Let us say that they know all of the latter's psychological and physical details just like the old Nepalese masseur, a deafmute, who for more than ten years has been at work early, every other morning, "to render supple that which needs to be," as the *Shofu* says. The ritual is precise. It lasts thirty minutes and ends with a resounding: "Thank you, Lorenza, thanks to you, I am combat-ready."

The choice of clothing is the domain of the President's sister and her private team, who spend a whole day every week on it; the choice—the first choice, the final decision—is Wei Shu's.

In the Palace, this selection time will be called the night ceremony repeated every Thursday evening. The designers dream about it. To be invited means being consecrated. Everything remains a secret until that moment, be it an international conference, a gala, a New Year's ceremony, or rare public discussions where the President appears in an outfit that bears "your" signature! "The most elegant woman in the world," according to the American *Vogue*, is wearing your creation… For the elect, this is really the beginning and the end of the world! In general, these people belong to the school of Laurence Xu, who was the first to bring Chinese haute couture into *Fashion Weeks* of the whole world. Half-legend, half-reality, it is said that this great creator was deeply affected by the colours in the frescos of the Mogao grottos, at the extremity of the Great Wall; not only the colors, but also the human silhouettes and costumes, drawn on the stone walls of that cave, from the seventh to the thirteenth century, inspire him. Xu transposes onto his creations what he saw in the profound countryside: the blue-greens of the Tangs and the Songs, the embroideries of the Misaos, the batiks of Anshun, the Yunjin brocades, lacework as delicate as butterfly skins discovered in nameless villages.

The President does not exaggerate with signatures. Nevertheless, she honors them, happy as she is to make known the ancestral skills, united with the most contemporary forms and materials. She has her favorites from among the vast array of Chinese fashion houses: Guo Pei for the special occasions; Uma Wang and Madame Min for everyday wear; Lu Kun who offers *hanfu*, roomy clothes for private receptions, for dinners with the *shifu* and relaxation.

A "six stars and beyond" service is assured twenty-four hours a day by these different staffs, who make up a total of two hundred people. Che Se keeps an eye on these disparate yet complementary teams who guarantee the reputation and ensure the quality of the first residence of China.

***

In the large library of the family's private residence, Che Se looks over again the next-day's program with the President, a program called "the first luminous day." The expression appears on all the official and unofficial documents: "the first luminous day."Commenting on this expression, in a message to his superiors, the American ambassador concludes: "Welcome to China on this first luminous day."

This language that certain European bloggers and diplomats call "precious" spread progressively across political Chinese literature under the influence of practices arising in Beijing. It thrusts its roots deep into history. Apparently, it is borrowed from the authors of the *Book of Odes*, published three thousand years ago. In that celebrated text, a constellation of terms revolves around the concept of harmony. These terms have forever impregnated Chinese minds and customs, literature and engravings. In it is described the law of heaven and its progressive seeping into the Chinese identity. In it reference is made to a marvellous country nearby yet never reached, within one's grasp but inaccessible. Hence this first luminous day!

The terms of this narrative are appealing. They are fair and powerful as was Houji, the founder of the Zhou dynasty. The son of a virgin who became pregnant after placing her footsteps within the gigantic ones of a god, he was abandoned by the roadside, at the mercy of beasts who did not approach him. And so he was left on an ice plain, in the belief that the strange child would not survive this abandonment. But hundreds of birds protected him from the cold with their feathers. Thus are born legends, myths and imaginary dynasties that traverse millenniums

Reinvented in every age, this story traces its source back to the narratives of those remote times which, in China, witnessed the birth of memory. It is said that in those times poetry and music constituted the levers of politics; education was the tool used for assimilation and not the possession of arms.

The term "luminous" chosen for this day is inscribed in this very ancient Chinese tradition, in this very ancient human tradition. It originates in the Zhou dynasty that was glorious more than three thousand years before, according to the Chinese calendar, and that stretched over nearly four millenniums. The country is indebted to the dynasty notably for the development of written language and an intense intellectual life.

The President likes to evoke those "creative moments in the history of China that have given birth to its legends, myths and traditions, moments that have shaped the nation's DNA." She knows this history well, out of personal interest and also as the heir of the great historian Jiang Sicong, her beloved mother, "my eternal friend," according to a phrase she often uses.

"You will have noticed, Che Se, that I am wearing my mother's long necklace of black pearls, a present from her father who had found it at an antique dealer's place in Kyoto. The latter got it from a distant cousin of the Emperor, a lady 'forsaken and impoverished' in the aftermath of the great war. It has become a kind of talisman in the family, a lucky charm. It is strange and perhaps premonitory, this lucky charm coming from Japan to China! It reminds me of my mother's elegance, her distinction, her unique beauty. I will wear it tomorrow in her honor in front of the whole world, with the silver necklace from the Miaos, a gift of the Assembly of Governors of our provinces. This gem, a marvel, illustrates the diversity of the country and the world."

Che Se regains control: "Madame President, tomorrow morning You will be devoted to recording your messages. Your will first address your compatriots in Putonghua Mandarin, their common language. Afterwards, you will address the population of the world in Hindi, Spanish, Arabic, then English. Your recording in the Chinese language will be made available at noon, followed thirty minutes later by your recordings available in the other languages."

This timetable and the choice of these languages are not without importance. China invested heavily during the whole 20th century to shape its common language; fusion and standardization of local and regional languages, with, as a reference, the Mandarin spoken in Beijing; transcription of the language, reorganization of writing in 1920, choice of the spoken language to the detriment of the former written one, specific provisions in the Constitution of 1982 ordering the use of Putonghua Mandarin in schools and institutions at all levels and for all official speeches in the public space.

Wei Shu always supported, politically and financially, the consolidation of this language both so ancient and new. "In order for their language to become the first in the world, it was necessary to ensure the success of this succession of reforms that created the language of the people of China." She considers this consolidation as "an essential and successful national project."

Launched by the Emperor Qin Shi Huangdi more than twenty-two centuries ago, the enterprise had been pursued since then in an intermittent manner. It was finally completed during the last few decades.

For the President, this marked a very great success for the regime, a success with considerable cultural, social and economic repercussions. "We have avoided the breakup that killed Latin in Europe and gave rise to a flowering of local languages." As a polyglot, she always addresses her audiences in Mandarin wherever she might be in the world, then, sometimes, takes pleasure in translating her words herself. At those times, she lets slip: "Allow me to be my own interpreter. This obliges me to think after having spoken to say the same thing in another way."

During this first luminous day, then, she has herself chosen to address the world in the three or four languages which, with Mandarin, "cover the planet extensively: Hindi, Spanish, Arabic and English."

Lunch will provide the opportunity to capture more intimate images transmitted in real time within the country and in the world. It will gather around the President her two children and her only sister, the family intendant and an Iranian friend, called the *shifu*, as he has been designated for the past fifteen years on the Web and in the international networks and medias. For some, he is "Mr. Wei Shu" of the uncertain status; for others, especially the popular medias, he is the bodyguard and the soul of the most beautiful woman in the world, "the friend who is so close that their shadows dance glued together," according to an Ivoirian blogger.

The couple is selectively discreet. Not much visible in China itself and never at the Party meetings, the gentleman nevertheless accompanies Madame during all her trips abroad. He is always by her side for the ceremonies of paramount importance and if the circumstances become difficult. Otherwise, according to urbane rumours emanating from the social networks, "he is at Madame's disposal, at her convenience."

For the photos and not for the food, the lunch will be held at Tian Xia Yan, one of the foremost restaurants in the arts 798 zone. At the turn of the new century, this unique zone in the heart of the Chinese capital, a former industrial complex and working-class district inspired by the Bauhaus style, was saved from demolition by artists and citizens supporting one another. Since then, the complex has become one of the stations for worldwide cultural creation.

Composed of multiple low, esthetically pleasing buildings, the ensemble has become a maze of workshops, galleries, studios, boutiques and restaurants.

"It will convey a '21st century mood,' festive and colorful," Che Se remarked.

"It will bring back beautiful memories, family dinners, dinners with my mother, birthday dinners, dinners among friends," Wei Shu continues.

"Dine with me," the *shifu* entreats.

Some dishes were prepared for the President and her guests: potatoes stuffed with bird nests and shredded chicken supreme with spiced mushrooms; braised pheasant supreme in a pot and bean sprouts; vegetarian rolls with bamboo shoots, vegetables in season, pickled vegetables, benzoin roots, and little "elephant eye" brioches which have always been on the presidential family table since Madame was three years old," he adds.

At 16h00, in the great hall of the People's Palace, the President would hold a multilingual press conference. It would be translated simultaneously and automatically in real time, in twelve languages, including Hindi, Swahili, Japanese, Korean, Haoussa, Vietnamese, Russian, English, Arabic, Spanish and French.

There would be present the members of the Political Bureau of the Permanent Committee of the Party, the members of the Central Military Commission that commands the three million five hundred thousand Chinese soldiers, the members of the government, the governors of the twenty-six provinces, the members of the Permanent Committee of the Representatives of the Central Party School, delegations from the Academy of Sciences and the Academy of Literature.

At 20h00, the one hundred and nine heads of state or government present in Beijing are invited to a formal dinner in the gardens of the Summer Palace, west of the capital. The President will speak there. She asked that a short address be prepared for her based on a quote that she finds inspiring for the occasion: "All the nations of the earth are the diversified embodiment of the same humanity." The President of Brazil will respond.

Sequences of this first days will be made available for television stations around the world and on the network of networks. Multilingual sites will relay, at a later time, the events of the first day of the reign of the President-Empress Wei Shu.

Che Se and his team ensure the monitoring of the images and messages. Probably never has the planet been inundated by such a profusion of images in a same day and relating to a same person.

From Peru to Nepal, from South Africa to Turkey, from Palestine to the Caribbean, the impact must embed its far- reaching effects everywhere in minds, memories and, why not, hearts. China's hour has returned. The great country is incarnated by this elegant, modern and multilingual woman. The tenth successor to Mao Zedong is moulded by national and international political experiences. Henceforth she commands the resources of the most powerful country in the world.

The message has been put together at length by the same team. No reference to the present circumstances, no concession to immediate events, no attack against the United States of America and the European Union. A futuristic stance by referring repeatedly to the challenges, but also to the assets.

Predictably, the gist of the message is centered on the prime, omnipresent idea of harmony. Although often betrayed, this banner has always been taken up again and carried by China, as far back as one can go in time.

Wei Shu puts her cards on the table by asking that the required texts be prepared emphasizing to the maximum the ancient proverb: *Step back and everything opens up spontaneously.*

"I wish to say enough so that our determination to rebuild the international system appears clearly; I wish to say it with words that are striking and expressions that last, but all the while taking into consideration the assets, exalting the plurality of the human family and adopting an inclusive position. Make sure that everything can be understood by the largest number of people. When preparing my speeches, use the technique of the ancient painters: have a grasp, a complete understanding of the subject, find where it fits into the unfolding of history and have recourse to techniques of expression that are the best adapted to my audiences. Find the words that create the right atmosphere, and consequently, remain in the memory."

Broken, low-pitched, Wei Shu's voice is her best weapon. At Party meetings, her adversaries as much as her allies look forward to her speeches. They are generally brief and constructed around only one theme and two or three precise proposals. Her flow is singular, as though she were making haste slowly. Her voice is not throaty, but "softly metallic," according to the *shifu*. Wherever she goes she has at her disposal powerful concoctions made available by classic Chinese medicine. Made with flour from the roots of old, dried red trees and leaves imported from Tibet, these concoctions "clear out what has to be cleared," as her friend says. According to him, "they give back to her voice the fullness which is, in itself, a message." Some say that this old recipe of Chinese medicine has served the orators of the Empire since before the construction of the Great Wall.

For the President, Chinese ancestral medicine has no equal. Her personal doctor is one of the most renowned specialists in this science that is based on the principle of treating life with life.

"I want everything I say to be understood by everyone, including the President of the United States. They call me "Lightning," in Washington. Let's prove them right by showing them what precedes lightning, calm wrested from the harshness of the elements. Harmony is this reconciliation of opposites, and truth, often the point where two contradictions meet. The West will never understand this superiority of our philosophy over theirs, based on separation and the elimination of opposites, just where we celebrate the incontestable power coming from the meeting of contrary fluxes."

***

The election of Wei Shu was "certain" for all the specialists of Chinese politics after the 21st Congress of the Party, in 2032. Finally acquired, but with difficulty, the renewal of her mandate as a member of the Central Committee represented a decisive victory over "tough and misogynistic adversaries." This renewal finally opened the doors, in 2034, to the Permanent Committee of the Party, that very first circle of power.

In her first speech before the Permanent Committee, Wei Shu maintained that she was "the choice of the representatives from the people's organisations and of a majority from the one hundred and twenty million Party members.

"Since the publication of my report *China in the 21st Century*, my speeches at the four last congresses of the Party, my participation in the dossiers dealing with the occupation of outer space, military affairs, cybernetic security and the setting up of new international institutions, I have experienced a fusion with the largest number of citizens, a resolute response to the proposals I developed with and for all of them.

"During these meetings that were often gigantic, I have tried to conduct myself as though in my village, at my grandparents' place.

11

There, on the public square, around the large table where one plays dice, everyone must listen to the elders who they themselves often evoke their own elders and the narratives of the latter. We were suddenly plunged deeply, very deeply into stories of famine, drought, volcanoes, births of triplets stuck to one another, clouds of birds that hide the skies, visitors emerging from the sea even though it was unknown here, stars brushing against the Earth and leaving there, for a while, an unforgettable light.

"Everyone speaks, but in turn. All can ask a question rather than contradict, show their disagreement by asking that the question be explained to them twice or three times. Few things are forbidden, except for the somewhat crazy great aunt who fled this universe where marriages were not meant to be happy but to last. Thus, from decade to decade, communities remained faithful to themselves, like particles of eternity.

"In short, everyone turns to their advantage the narrative based on the anecdotes of the day or the exploits of the ancestors. I carry within my memory the precious belief that, in this village, each person takes care of the others, as my grandmother said hundreds of times. All my life I have been driven by this strange feeling of betraying or implementing the primary objective of taking care of others.

"I declare here, at the table of this Committee, my feeling of deep pride in belonging to the longest ever human history, the history of the Chinese people; my infinite admiration for what this people has contributed to universal civilization and for what we have accomplished during the past two generations, since the revolution, this impossible and yet successful transition: from the biggest of the poorest countries, we have become the foremost economic power in the world. Here are the reasons why I am committed to the Party, why I am committed to my country, these inseparables."

The events leading to the new President's taking of office had been carefully prepared months before. Under the appearance of spontaneity, each sequence of this first day is planned as a major event in itself that is enhanced by a precise framework constructed and scripted according to the audiences targeted.

Thus, for recording the President's messages, images selected showing her in Brazil, in Germany, in the United States, in Japan, in Europe, in the Federation of Gulf States, in India and China will accompany her talks to the audiences for which they are destined.

Her dressers and stylists must be aware of these images and take them into account. "Harmony is in everything, and everything is in harmony," the cabinet director repeats to his teams.

The lady likes "straight" clothes, as she says. "No bell shapes, no panniers, no umbrellas. I like everything that is close to the body. I do not wish in the least to resemble the last queen of England, always squeezed within colored wrappings."

A silk-like skin, a face open at all times, a tall demeanor made fluid by years of di gong and yoga. The President exercises under the guidance of a trainer who is a disciple of Patanjali, the author of that treatise about two thousand years old combining a maximum of proposals and a minimum of words. The hairdressers and makeup artists are discreet, bold and classic, according to the boss' mood, the circumstances surrounding her appearances and the successive environments. According, as well, to the orders received from the entourage and the *shifu*, who attends to everything, judges everything, decides on everything when dealing with the "outward appearance" of the President. In some cases, careers are called into question, and all of those people who move in the environment of the "Empress" know it!

For the lunch in the 798 arts zone, the famous installation by Chen Shaofeng titled *People Without a Voice*, exhibited for the first time in 2003 at the Alexander Ochs Private Gallery in Berlin, was moved into the *Beijing White Space*.

On multiple little white surfaces stand out, one by one, the hundreds of beautiful and grave faces of male and female peasants from the village of Tiangongsi, in the province of Hubei. For each one, a photo and a drawing represent them and deepen the mystery of these modest and dignified beings.

On the way to Tian Xia Yan, the President will make a brief stop there. Under the gazes of these hundreds of doubled faces, she will make a brief statement. "This is what we are no longer, she will say, a country made up of rich and powerful megacities, and a vast rural zone that is poor and weak. China has put an end to this profound and tragic fracture in our country. These faces remind us of where we come from and the immense effort our Party has accomplished these past decades."

For the press conference, a gigantic tapestry was commissioned that represented the different regions of the world. On examining it,

Che Se had fun pointing out the regions of the "near, middle and extreme Occident," mocking the colonial language with its Near, Middle and Extreme Orient. "The Empress" will be seated in front of the gigantic work to meet the international press.

"Henceforth, declares the *shifu*, one will not be able to see her without also seeing the world in its entirety."

Finally, for the official dinner that will be offered to the heads of state and government, immense translucid screens partition the esplanade surrounding the Spacious Pavilion, one of the most spectacular buildings within the Summer Palace. The guests will number there in the hundreds. Throughout the reception, will be projected the architectural beauties of this immense domain of two hundred and ninety hectares created in the 12th century and constantly enriched since then. The Great monumental arch, the famous East Gates, those of Kindness, of the Moon and the Scattering of Clouds. The Pavilions of the Jade Whirlpool, of the Lotus Perfume, of the Declining Light, of the Harmony of Earth and Water, and of Longevity will also be shown. Finally, will be shown the Great Theatre, the Long Promenade, the Towers of Buddha and other marvels such as the exquisite boat of purity, the famous bronze lions and the fantastic granite beasts that protect the imperial domain.

During the whole dinner will be heard the classic musical compositions of the country, those, as the program explains, that benefited from the music bureau created by the Emperor Qin twenty-three centuries ago and from the institutions that developed as a result of that impetus. Following musical compositions from the minorities will come those of the golden ages performed on ancient citharas with seven and twenty strings. Cascades of harmony will flow through vindicating that god who defined Chinese music as "a poetry without words."

The choice of this location where "are brought together all of the beauties of nature and of human creation" is not fortuitous. It embodies the duration of Chinese civilization, its millennial ability to blossom forth again and to plunge its worst ordeals into the shadows of the past. This great domain is a spectacular illustration of it.

On two occasions, it was reduced to ashes; by the French forces in 1800 and, in 1900, by the forces of the eight allied powers that occupied the Chinese capital. The Dowager Empress Cixi ordered the reconstruction of the Summer Palace and of the hundreds of buildings and sites that composed it. The greatest architects of the time were asked to insert the buildings within the natural beauties of the mountain of longevity and to make sure their mobile reflections would appear in the large expanses of water of the Jade Lake.

***

The day is a resounding success. Wei Shu returns by helicopter to her residence near the Forbidden City. She enjoys "this tour of Beijing which is a tour of history, because the three areas that encircle the imperial complex appear in such a perfect geometrical order. The Chinese City that shelters the temple of heaven closes the vast territory and leads to the Tartar City, which itself empties into the Imperial City. And, at the heart of this trilogy enclosed by a pink wall, are the pavilions, gardens, expanses of water and palaces reserved for the imperial family and built around the imperial throne."

At her residence, she takes a call from a close friend who is in Berlin, goes in to say goodnight to her grandchildren and retires to her suite.

Here she is alone with her *shifu*.

She puts on a superb lilac tunic embroidered with delicate lotus flowers of silver thread. The effect is gripping for its beauty, certainly, but also for its symbol, since this flower, for thousands of years in China, has suggested the fertility of bodies as well as minds. She wears her long necklace of black pearls and a ring set with an emerald, her favorite precious stone. The *shifu* slipped it on her finger this morning while murmuring only: "This will be a superb moment." He takes her in his arms, embraces her for a long time, then does it once again, holding her even longer. She takes his face between her hands. He pushes her back gently. "Let me contemplate you for a moment." She rushes into a rare monologue, intimate, disconnected, a mixture of fatigue, emotions and memories, in this unique moment of her life. Shu is unstoppable.

"A bouquet of thankyous, my dear friend, for what you have been for me for so long and what you will be in future times. You know, this evening, I keep thinking of my mother, a beautiful young woman, a beautiful old one, so beautiful always, yet modest, but scholarly, the greatest historian in the country, recognized here, universally recognized. Her collar of black pearls has not left me, these past few days. How happy she would be to share this moment with you and me.

"I have been thinking of her all day long. At the luncheon, in this cultural neighborhood she frequented until her death; at the press conference, where I had the feeling that she was whispering the right words to me; at the dinner, in this palace the history of which she related marvellously.

"In the great hall of the Jade Pavilion, I saw her shadow pass. She seemed to me both frightened and happy to see her little flower at the head of the country and the world. She drew near, then vanished. I searched for her in vain. But at least I saw again for a fleeting moment her face immediately swallowed up by the void.

"You know, I have told you this already, she used to tuck us in herself. She used to envelop us in the warmth of the sheets and in her affection. She would make herself a seat with comfortable cushions at the foot of the bed and would launch into extraordinary narratives. I didn't know then that these were portions of our history adapted for the hearts and minds of us children. Not surprising coming from her!

"Thus, as a very little child, I listened to the history of the origins of all things, the history of what was before the origins, of what was 'at the time when the uncreated occupied the whole of space.'

"This narrative, my mother would tell us, comes to us from Siberia and from so far back in time that the addition of centuries appears light in comparison to that interminable duration. From Siberia, the history of the origins migrated over to us, then to Japan and the whole of Asia. It has lived and continues to live in the memories of billions of living souls who have heard it since the beginnings of all things.

"Much later, I understood that this history followed not only the physical trajectory of Taoism, but also its spiritual one. The narrative of this apparent void takes into consideration not only the physical dimension of the world, but also the other, impalpable and yet very real dimension of that which is alive. I understood today, during this uninterrupted succession of ceremonies, that we inhabit the first and that the second inhabits us."

Night stretches out. Wei Shu continues.

"My dear friend, you know, I have thought one hundred times today about the story of Fuxi, the first sovereign of China. My mother told us this story with felicitous or dramatic variations, according to the dominant emotion of the time.

"Fuxi reigned for so long that this distance is compared to that of the unreachable ocean depths. Everything came with this king, she told us, everything came from this king: agriculture and writing, iron smelting and craftmanship, plus the rules by which men are governed. He had the rare gift of connecting ideas to the things that embody them. He was like the musician who first hears the melody within him then enables the masses to hear it.

"The story of Fuxi is beautiful. This king, our mother told us, planted our whole history, and all our stories like some great invisible forest within our minds and hearts. Since that time, we have been striving to see this forest, to encompass it. But then we discover that it is not only invisible, but also mobile.

Some people withdraw into themselves, convinced that the forest and its mysteries are within them and that they constitute with it a unique being. Others keep their distances. The latter endeavour to establish footbridges between their intimate world and this invisible and mobile forest, like two spheres waiting for one another, indispensable for one another, each one incomplete without the other. I know today that these incursions into the history of Fuxi summarize centuries of human thought in our country. Westerners would have made him a disciple of Plato or even of his old man, Socrates, I think...

"But, at the time, our child-like imaginations were completely absorbed by the personage of this first king of China. Did he not have treasures in his big bag, especially words, plants, iron that was liquid then congealed in vases, weapons, sieges and other conveniences? Our imagination was impregnated with unreachable ocean depths, with this invisible and mobile forest lodged within the heart and mind of certain people, and also with footbridges leading to this impossible forest. We would draw this forest for hours on end. Mother used to say: "There could be a little more light. Where are the nests for the birds? And why this big black hat on your trees squeezed against one another?" Sometimes, she would add a skyline, a bit of shade, a vermillion stroke, a kiss on our foreheads and a big resounding goodnight.

"It was as though these stories haunted me all day. A voice in me kept telling me that, as the President, I was henceforth in the tradition of Fuxi, in that long chain of services rendered to the great people of China. I could feel him by my side. It seemed to me that he was observing my gestures, evaluating my words, looking in the same direction I was and closing his eyes when I would close mine.

"You know, President Tang had me wear an extraordinary present yesterday, the imperial seal used by the Emperor Kangxi, in the 17th century. I will place it on my desk at the residence."

Tonight, the President and her *shifu* sacrifice their traditional game of Chinese checkers, this ancient game which Wei Shu learned to play in the village, at her maternal grand-parents home.

"Tonight, you must rest, my beloved. We'll play two games tomorrow, if you want.

"You know, all the villagers would come to the square, near the big table where card, checkers or chess games took place. They would surround the players and acclaim the winners. I have learned a great deal from these ancients: the manipulation of silences; impatience and its opposite, cunning; the rhythms of victory and of vengeance, immediate and often fleeting in the first case, slow and durable in the second.

"At nightfall, everyone went home filled with a simple and common joy. There was a large house enclosed by walls, it was ours, with two or three courtyards, and all the others were made of straw and lime, with fat spiders and vermin that fed on their eggs. We would strike them with little leaf brooms or we would ruin them with thick smoke, if the evening was cold. In the families, everybody, male and female, would sleep in the same room from which suddenly emerged whispers, laughter or sometimes sobs.

"Back in Beijing, we would reminisce about those happy moments spent in the village. There would be the gathering of melons at the end of the day; the fishing for carp at the base of the falls of the nice or crazy stream, according to the seasons; the spectacular games of cards, checkers and chess that went on late into the night, the evenings of duels between village teams of the township; then the crackling of firecrackers that marked the end of the festival and that, according to my two grandmothers, chase away the evil spirits. Tonight, this crackling was heard in thousands of districts and cities throughout the country. They, too, marked the end of the festival. Let us hope that they have driven out the evil spirits of the world.

"Don't forget tomorrow to send an offering to the Dongyue temple. Four guardians have been protecting the four points of the compass there for centuries. As my mother, who regularly deposited victuals there, said: we needed them yesterday and we will need them tomorrow. Sleep well. I love you."

"Me too, Madame, on this first, our first presidential night. I love you, too."

CHAPTER II

WEI SHU, MINISTER AND DIPLOMAT

THE DAUGHTER-IN-LAW OF PRESIDENT FANG AS WELL AS A RENOWNED economist, a supporter of the historical study of the Chinese mindset and a reformer within the Party, Wei Shu has been in office for more than a quarter of a century. Named head of the Ministry for Economic Planning and Development in 2025, she had already cleared a succession of stages or tests in the Party and in the government, until the ministerial appointment to which would be added, in 2034, that of member of the Party's Permanent Committee. To rise to one of those functions is already a political exploit; to rise to two signifies being a dominant force on the podium.

Such a position is fraught with peril. A success achieved in the Party or government does not necessarily carry over from one sphere to another, whereas failure *per se* is contagious. The moment is also full of risks. Indeed, the balances between the vast sector of State-run companies and the no less impressive private sector are complex from the triple point of view of the tax system, the financing of research, and national and international investment. If the complementarities are significant, they still must come to terms with numerous disparities in national and international as well as political and economic interests. The apparent harmony between the two spheres cannot hide these disparities.

The minister must arbitrate between these interests by taking into consideration the demands of the Party, the decisions of the government, the requirements of a service economy for one billion three hundred million people, those also of the productive sectors of the economy, and the demands of international commerce.

In this impossible position, Wei Shu will emerge as a redoubtable negotiator. The "First Mandarin," as she is called in Beijing at that time, has at her disposal a seemingly inexhaustible reserve of formulas, compromises, settlement proposals that it is better to accept unless one wishes to "enter the zone of perpetual regret."

***

Within the Party, this expression assured Wei Shu a favorable vote in her fight to abolish the death penalty, except for crimes linked to national security. "You have the choice: either you enter into history, or you enter the zone of perpetual regret." The next day, hundreds of colleagues received this simple message: "Thank you for having chosen history. Wei."

In international financial institutions, people dread her, because her demonstrations leave her interlocutors as though lost in the face of references that are totally foreign to them.

In Geneva, where China's position on the improbable relaunching of the World Trade Organization was anticipated impatiently, she evokes the 1895 Treaty of Shimonoseki between China and Japan, its long-term effects until the fall of the Chinese Empire in 1912, twenty-two centuries old at the time.

Although enjoying a large majority around the big negotiating table, the Westerners felt lost.

"What is that Chinese woman talking about? The British representative had asked of his neighbor.

--Here she is, that Chinese woman, Mr. Ambassador. It is better to turn off one's microphone in order to avoid displaying one's ignorance."

Then she drowned them literally by drawing up the new map of Asia resulting from this treaty. Taiwan, a Dutch colony in the 17th century that became Japanese again, this time around; Korea, a protectorate dominated by Kyoto; Manchuria, a special zone at the disposal of the Japanese for commerce and investment. "One must see far, very far behind and ahead, before committing one's country."

The following year, at the table of the Security Council, Wei Shu was referring to the "two great world wars" in terms that were incomprehensible for many of her colleagues. She evoked the explosion of a bomb on the railway track, at the Moukden station, as the trigger unleashing the war which would propel the Chinese Communist Party to power and, in time, change the world. After ten minutes of a speech of which she accepted the consequences, she conjured up the two wars that had inflamed Asia. The conflicts of 1904-1905 and of 1931-1945 which had both pitted Japan against China over Manchuria had drawn in almost all the countries of East Asia and Central Asia, then Russia that had become in the interval the USSR. Here were the two great world wars as the Asian narrative viewed them, according to Wei Shu.

One day, at the Security Council, she had replied sharply to Lord Steward, Great Britain's arrogant ambassador, in a way that made a majority of Google users gasp: "Tell your government that as far as one can see in the centuries to come, it will never be able to impose a second Peace of Shimonoseki on my country." The English diplomat replaced his toupee and walled himself up in silence, fully aware that one more word out of line would bring upon him a second thrashing, like the one the ambassador of France endured: "Your speeches are very, too, long, Mr. Ambassador. You are familiar with our proverb: *One mouse dropping is enough to spoil a large kettle of soup...* All you need is one word..."

Before it became normal, she overturned the geopolitical references that used to dominate the arguments of Western representatives by substituting other ones: the ones that marked modern and contemporary history "where the human majority lives." She had explained herself in clear terms.

"In our time, another account of History already unfolded and about to unfold is emerging and will in the end replace the propaganda machine that has been feeding minds for at least two centuries. Every river has two banks. The human majority shares ours.

"Artistic expressions coming from different cultures, including Asian cultures, ours, but also those of Africa, those of the Arab-speaking world, so rich, as well as those of the indigenous nations of the world have forever been presented as exotic curiosities. What a reduction, what a negation of humanity's common cultural heritage! Now you know why I organized this large colloquium at the United Nations—to celebrate the one thousand three hundred years of the Imperial Academy of Music, created in 735 by the Emperor Tang Xuanzong. No mention whatsoever, in encyclopedias, histories of music, systems of reference in all the Googles of the western world of a cultural thrust which was decisive for several billion human beings!

"The same holds true in the scientific and technological domains. On this issue, I often quote Joseph Needham, the greatest western specialist in Chinese civilization and a close friend of my father. In his work *Science in Traditional China*, he writes: 'The long succession of technical discoveries that took place in China was almost entirely passed over in silence in scholarly texts and others in the field.' Our friend Needham set up the inventory of the Chinese contribution to man's understanding and mastery of nature, and, according to his findings, it was a great contribution. No people, he added, has enjoyed the monopoly of scientific development, and all achievements must be recognized and celebrated if we want to pursue our path towards universal fraternity and harmony.

"I myself heard, at the family table, the famous Cambridge researcher assert that the continuous transmission of Chinese techniques towards the West was of vital importance for Europe. Western pride has completely eradicated the names and the contributions of the great scientists of my country, including the astronomer Guo Shoujing, who, in the 13ᵗʰ century, uncovered the secret of the daily movement of the stars; the geographer Pei Xiu, who revolutionized his domain by developing squared grids; Liu Hui, in the 13ᵗʰ century, who laid the foundations of modern Chinese mathematics, the matrices of universal mathematics. The West's hegemonic will explains this drifting of the mind, this crime against truth and history. One more step and we will create the void. We must rewrite the history of sciences by recognizing the magnitude of all such contributions.

"In the family library, my mother kept a collection of ancient books that bear witness to China's contribution to the creation of universal science. I have retained this collection. It contains many works covering more than two thousand years of research, experiments and contributions to universal science. I have in mind a certain number of them that I have examined very carefully. I am thinking of *The Internal Canon of the Yellow Emperor*, written twenty-two centuries ago and which constitutes the basis of our medicine. It boasts the very first essay that classifies plants and animals, and the very first treatise on alchemy. The collection also contains an encyclopedia published in the 12ᵗʰ century, which synthesizes the sciences of the time; a thousand-year-old incunable which is one of the oldest treatises on architecture in history. I have leafed through it more than a hundred times. I also recall the fifty volumes of a large collection of architecture published in the 16th century during the reign of the Emperor Yong-Thing. From that period, my mother cherished the original edition of perhaps the most famous play in our classical repertory: *The Pavilion of Peonies*. She also spoke about her discovery of the Four Extraordinary Books: *The Kingdoms; At the Water's Edge; The Peregrination Towards the West* and *Jin Ping Mei*.

"Here, then, are the materials, from among so many, that are at the heart of our intention. To recreate the narrative of history. To welcome these remarkable contributions that have served as the foundations of Chinese culture and science within the culture and science of humanity. To see finally history as a vast score the interpretation of which calls for the participation of the whole orchestra, of all the instruments, each one judged indispensable. And, consequently, to put an end to the intellectual and political hoax that has reduced history to the events which have unfolded on European territory or from European territory, and, during the modern and contemporary period, has relativized conquered territories and enslaved populations in all parts of the world. You have grown accustomed to observing the spark, you will henceforth be obliged to get used to contemplating the sun!"

This girl from the north-east of China became known for hundreds of these polished formulas. For an extreme politeness as well—"Your enemies will forever hold a grudge against you for being too polite," she would repeat to her assistants—and for an implacable toughness— "I am very grateful to you for having allowed us access to the dark side of your mind. We did not know that it was so degraded." The American lady ambassador to the United Nations, to whom this provocative formula was addressed, was still searching for a reply five years after the incident.

***

Already considered one of the most influential people in the international community, her appointment, in 2027, as Head of the Mission to the UN of the Popular Republic of China had catapulted her to the first international political platform and had as a result increased her visibility on a worldwide scale.

"They are sending me away from Beijing, but I will return there. Such is the rule for all diplomats. Such is my will as well. It is here, in my adopted city, that I like to practice qi gong in the parks. Elsewhere, except in the South African city of the Cape—and I cannot tell you why—I do not experience the capital gain of balance and harmony from the energy-giving flows of the yin and the yang that the practice of qi gong normally brings. Here, the city regenerates me every day."

Wang Jing, the most widely read blogger in China, had written right on the day after the appointment of Wei to New York: "The Ambassador Wei Shu missing the energy-giving flows that practicing politics in Beijing brings announces her return even before her departure. This is high class post-Olympic tai-chi."

Her move to New York, in 2027, had followed the election of her father-in-law to the presidency of the Popular Republic, in the preceding year.

Was it a concession to her adversaries within the Party?

Was it the personal choice of the new President to reinforce the international stature of the divorced wife of his oldest son who had been, still was, and would be among the most faithful to him politically?

Was it an offensive launched by the government of Beijing to accelerate the transformation of international institutions according to the new geopolitical circumstances and China's national interests?

"A bit of all three, she declares to the Press Club of the United Nations. And perhaps as well the realization that I have a certain talent when it comes to negotiating, this time put into service to reform international institutions, which have been paralyzed for at least two decades. Is it necessary to reform them, revitalize them, replace them? Is there still fire in these volcanos?"

From her very first speech at the General Assembly, "The Lightning Bolt" had struck and struck hard, as it was wont to do during moments of heightened tension at the Central Committee.

"Are you familiar with the story of the coolie who writes his destination in his hat then, unthinking and irresponsible, throws it into the sea? Do not imitate him, my dear colleagues, or you, too, will risk not knowing your destination."

The exegetes had quickly deciphered the message: the destination meant the alliance with the Middle Kingdom.

Negotiated word for word with Beijing, this discourse clarified, in a few formulas, the purpose of her mandate and her action in New York.

The countries of the world no longer define themselves in relationship with the United States and its presumed allies whose military, financial and economic

25

partnerships are in tatters. These times have been behind us for at least three decades. The institutions that bear their signatures and have reflected the petty and aggressive interests of that country since the middle of the last century, have become obsolete. The historical narrative carried by powers of another era has also become obsolete.

If its scientific, technological and military advances, if its currency and diplomacy have dominated the world, this past century, this is no longer the case today. Such will not be the case as far ahead as one can see in the times to come.

Certainly, the United States of America are not devoid of means. The latter however no longer allow them to define and dictate unilaterally the common rules of which the family of nations has a pressing need. They are no longer able to impose their norms on everyone and transgress them without restraint.

Mr. Ambassador of the United States of America, my government and so many others in the world that are represented here, have lost whatever confidence they still could have in your country in the recent past, which has become archaic for the times to come, after having been bellicose in times past. As always happens when one is weak, you have become archaically bellicose.

What must one evoke for you to liberate yourselves from the illusions which you entertain about what you are, what you represent, what you no longer are, what you no longer represent?

Impoverished in all respects, your people are the first social and economic victims of a policy of another time, the American people as well as those whose governments still find themselves associated with your archaic imperial system.

Henceforth, you will find China and her allies along your road. We know, you know that our vision and policies that embody it are shared by a majority of Member States of the United Nations, a majority of the people of this world. Tomorrow, this is our conviction, it will be the common reference of all humanity.

"The applause, she related, could be heard all the way to Washington."

That evening, at the famous Waldorf-Astoria Hotel, a property of a Chinese insurance company since October 2014, Wei Shu had offered the first in a long series of receptions that would be the most sought after by the diplomatic community in New York. Her invitation cards were anticipated, kept, collected. On them were engraved, in red, representations of the four social virtues: the Li, the Yi, the Lian and the Tchi – propriety, justice, integrity and honor. "She absorbs all the light and sends it back to anyone she chooses", writes the journalist of the *Frankfurter Allgemeine Zeitung.*

"The lightning bolt" had transformed herself into a sophisticated, vibrant, warm hostess. Draped in a red and black sheathed dress, her favorite colors, she would move from one salon to the other, greeting her guests the way one greets personal friends, old acquaintances finally found again.

Friends, may you be thanked for being with us tonight. Every river has two banks. This afternoon, we have celebrated the new era which, by common acknowledgement, calls for a new policy and new common and shared institutions.

This evening, we find ourselves on the other bank. As I speak to you at this very moment, my government is announcing in Beijing the convening of a series of international conferences devoted to the stakes and the challenges in the world today, including technological and spatial security; the conservation and production of water on a planetary scale; the financing of world-wide sanitary protection and finally the rebuilding of the international system. Be thanked again for being with us… And let the celebration begin!

***

"The Lightning Bolt" had struck a second time in the same day. China could boast of a redoubtable emissary in New York. In this symbolic city of America, she exulted confidently and repeated to anyone who was willing to listen: "New York the magnificent has dominated the 20th century; Shanghai does and will do the same in the present century."

Sought out, her presence enhanced dinners, conferences, concerts, and followed a whole arsenal of rituals. Wei Shu would arrive before everyone else and metamorphosed herself into the second hostess of the evening, or she would be the last to arrive and have herself escorted to the very centre of the action under the gaze of all the audience.

The celebrated New York blogger Blanche Cochrane summed up the opinion of many people when she wrote:

The head of the Chinese Mission dominates even when she is not there. Everyone wonders why she did not come, whom she might have greeted first, what statements she might have sent, with her accustomed style and discretion, and that laptops would immediately bring to the attention of all the chancelleries and publications that count. She exists even when she is not there, until the moment she makes her entrance, touching off right away another volley of rumors, suppositions and speculations. These fifteen minutes of a late presence are transformed into innumerable messages on the American and international networks, namely, the Chinese one, which Madame Ambassador sets aside for privileged moments of encounter. Each one verifies if she has mentioned such or such a person in her short messages relayed to her one hundred and forty million subscribers on the most familiar microblogging platform, because her silences weigh heavily on the negotiations that are unfolding, on the agendas, political tides carrying rumors, truths, hypotheses, tactical fragments and other intangible items. They say she has practiced this method all her life, as much in the Party as in the government! A permanent whim for some, a strategy planned in the most minute detail for others, perhaps. But, for all the envoy from Beijing is a star who chooses her firmaments. Dixit Blanche Cochrane.

Being rare, her mediatic interviews are always astonishing. She lets out evaluations that make an impact as well as the headlines. One day she declared to the newspaper *Le Monde:*

"I am in love with the Arabic civilization, one of the most refined in the world, along with the Chinese. From language to history, from philosophy to trade, our links are ancient. They had become dull, but we have recently given them a real youth cure.

"You know about my passion for contemporary painting. I have great painters from the Arab-speaking space in my collection. You are familiar with Mahi Binebine—I contemplate his works the way believers venerate the Holy Scriptures—and Dia Azzawi, who from Bagdad depicted the Arab subconscious in dazzling colors. I have the same passion for the African civilizations that we have been rediscovering since the turn of this century. I also have in my collection great African painters, including the Congolese Bouvy Enkobo, for whom I have a preference. He is the finest colorist since our own Zhao Mengfu!

"We also have very ancient links with the African sub-Sahara, as bear out the archeological digs on the eastern coasts of the continent. They have found porcelain bowels which are as old as your Notre-Dame. It is said that these were exchanged for exotic animals, notably giraffes. During this past half-century, our links with the Africans have been revived and enriched substantially, our economies and our trade have become interdependent, and our main institutions work in synergy in all the areas that count. We can predict that within fifteen years the China-Africa trade will occupy the first place in many sectors of international exchanges. On the political level, our consultations go on continuously and our interventions are convergent. In short, our relations are exemplary."

Without taking precautions, she declared one day to the *O Estado* of Sao Paulo that "the treatment of the Indigenous people by the Europeans constitutes a series of genocides without equivalent in history, an incredible execution of tens of millions of people, of hundreds of communities, of languages and cultures."

Of this America—where she was living "in exile for a time—she would celebrate "the lost vitality, a consequence of its blindness and of the development of a racist ecosystem that has invaded everything, minds, medias, political parties, social networks, courts and laws, and all that on all levels, from Washington to the city hall of the smallest abandoned Texan village."

But, she reminds us:

"This country welcomed Antonin Dvorak and thus made possible the creation of the *Symphony from The New World,* that moving acknowledgement of vibrant yet suffering identities. It also allowed Jackson Pollock to show and celebrate the distant inner landscape of the world. Finally, it was here, in rejoicing and sorrow, that Jean-Michel Basquiat set up a disquieting and luminous inventory of the dramas lived by the black nation of this country and the world. The poster of his exhibit in Florence in 1983 has my preference. The intensity of the gazes initiates us into what the artist sees and what we, we cannot see."

Wei Shu also likes to refer to the era of the *negro spirituals,* those summaries of the drama of slavery, of exile, of suffering, of radical alienation and of ultimate liberation that was still to come. From memory, she quotes with precision the oldest of these works, underlines their raw truth, those moaning strains where are mingled, in the memories and the bodies, the hot winds of Africa and the whiplash-like cold of America. There were, thus, unspeakable abuses and tenacious yet faint hopes, life and death, everything that links them and everything that separates them. She draws bold parallelisms between these works and classical Chinese poetry: "I observe there the same distance, the same affliction, similar clusters of disappointments and, although apparently fragile, imperishable disappointments."

I never stop thinking about my country,
My heart is bruised from it,
Why can't I be the fragile bird
Who returns to his land.

"Who, then, wrote this simple and magnificent text? she had asked one day a curator of the Metropolitan Museum in New York. A slave from South Carolina in the 19th century or the princess Si-Kivu sent off, more than twenty centuries ago, to the north-west extremity of China by her father, the Emperor Han Wudi, to marry the heir apparent to the throne of the barbaric kingdom of Wasun?"

29

In her large apartment on Fifth Avenue "under surveillance by the FBI twenty-four hours a day, seven days a week, even if it is scanned electronically at regular intervals," she would receive, dressed in a *qipao* or a *changshan,* everyone who mattered in politics, diplomacy, economics and culture and living in that "redoubtable capital of the world." Then there were the other dinners, often "among the girls," those which had taken place with the women heads of diplomatic missions in New York, the expected ones and the others, like the dinner of her dreams: to her right, Maya Angelou and to her left, Fang Fang, the author of *A Splendid View,* then Marguerite Yourcenar, Wang Anyi, Mary Higgins Clark, Aminata Dramane Traoré and Toni Morrison. She had dreamt of this dinner with those immaterial girlfriends whose writings she used to read and reread. She always wondered what their encounters, conversations, silences, laughter, embarrassment, shared doubts, parallel perspectives would have produced, but which, in her dreams, converged progressively.

At her place she also invited guests to movie screenings. She loved to "get people to love" the great Chinese classics as well as some American films including an old one that she preferred, *The Good Luck Club* by the director Wayne Wang, with the actors and actresses Ming-Na, Russell Wong, Lisa Lu, France Nuyen. "Here is a remarkable exception. They were talking about us in intelligent terms," she said. Just as in the novel by Amy Tan."

The truth is that she was getting bored in New York. In a letter to her father, she had opened up her heart on the matter:

I miss every day the street sounds and smells of Beijing, the crowd everywhere and at all times, the little houses of the old neighborhoods of the city, what is left of them, the street food, the words and accents that float in the air. During evenings of depression, I long for the beauty of the vast rice fields of the delta of the Yangzi as seen from an airplane, on days of bright sunlight. I also miss contributing up close to the formidable élan of the country. Here, everything is geared to clumsily preserving what was once the élan of America and which no longer exists.

***

The day after her election to the most important political position on the planet, in 2036, the world medias will have the choice of angles from which to analyze the character, the ideas, the career, the measured extravagances of this sixty-year-old woman, divorced, mother of two children who, according to her, "have recycled themselves into our abnormal life; one by producing historical documentaries, the other, by working in national archeology. My mother and her mother would be delighted."

In a rare expansive moment, she had confided to the *Guardian* that had prepared a portrait of Wei Shu, Diplomatic Mission Head at the United Nations:

"I wished to develop in them a capacity to be engaged: I did not bring them into the world to worry but to fulfill themselves. From their adolescence onwards I have taken them to the governing bodies of the Party, these important places where the real China and the idealized China, China and the world meet; these important places where the flow of time links ancient unresolved challenges and the ones that the human adventure continuously constructs.

"There is nothing they do not know about the struggles, alliances, abandonments and compromises that forge political life and bring out its meaning. Some never recover from it entirely since decision-making is so demanding. In these places are defined the orientations and choices which will affect one billion three hundred million people and, for an ever-increasing number of issues, the whole of humanity.

"I have also endeavored to initiate them into the rites which are at the heart of the Chinese mind-set. I love our ancient texts. The writings of Mencius inspire me. His conviction that righteousness-kindness, or *renyi*, constitutes the foundation of the world and of our minds; that shame and justice are interdependent and that the notion of the good one experiences is the beginning of wisdom, all of this has always nourished my thinking.

"Yes, I read and reread our ancient texts: *The Book of Odes, The Conversations of Confucius, The Book of Mencius,* the *Zhuangzi,* by Tchouang-tseu, but also the *Song of Chu,* that comprises the poems of Qu Yuan. My mother used to read us excerpts from them as well as from the *Annales of Springs and Autumns* and from the famous *Historical Memoirs* by Sima Qian.

"I feel sad, very sad when I think that the West has no knowledge of all these riches. How is this possible?

"All these authors do not have the same conception of singular human life, of human life as a community and of human life within the nation, of human life everywhere on this Earth. They have all enlightened, however, in their way, the cyclical character of all that happens in the Universe, this fundamental fact. In that sense, they are all architects of the diversity and the maturity of our patrimony. Through the centuries, they have produced the essence of our DNA and the foundations of our indispensable solidarity. Such are the feelings of those who have frequented their works and, by so doing, have acquired the conviction of belonging and contributing to our civilization. Finally, as a privilege of immaterial riches, they must navigate from mind to mind, this obligatory transition towards responsibility."

The journalists of *The Guardian* had not asked for so much. They made the front page with this far-reaching conversation and a photo of Wei Shu with her two children in front of the three great pyramids of Gizeh constructed about five thousand years before. She sent them her assessment in a brief and heartfelt hand-written note:

China and Egypt were in communication with one another when these pyramids were constructed, and the thinking of their respective sages were already enriching one another. This is what I have told my children when contemplating with them these extraordinary human achievements.

CHAPTER III

WEI SHU, FROM BEIJING TO NEW YORK TO BEIJING

CERTAIN MEDIAS FAVOR WEI SHU'S DIPLOMATIC CAREER AND STRIVE TO decipher the alchemy that links the utmost politeness and the most implacable toughness. They speculate about her genuine interest for this "chair" work, according to one of her enigmatic statements. Certainly, at the United Nations she has a large theatre at her disposal and reinvents her role there every day.

Surrounded by her bodyguards, she criss-crosses New York and the glass palace as though they were her private domains, willingly makes the work of journalists and other paparazzi easier, seizes every opportunity to make the *front page* in America, or *tou ban* in China.

She makes herself scarce, then omnipresent. She disappears and reappears, is present where one expects her, but also where one does not expect her. "Reclusion is not the contrary of presence. It is the primary condition of the other. I exercise it in my private as well as in my political life. Suddenly, those who appreciate you, but also those who fear you become anxious. The return is rarely banal."

Her sallies are choreographed carefully. The Office, as her personal team is called, arranges for her to be expected, welcomed, accompanied, applauded. Her appearances are captured and retransmitted on all the medias of her lifelong ally, the Tencent group, according to a method perfected by President Deng who combined the "three Ps": permanency, pertinence, proximity of the images and the commentary and their integration into the most up-to-date newscasts. She is well established in one of the most influential news ecosystems on the planet and present in all the others. If, in New York, the presence at her side of the person called the *shifu* is more and more constant, there is nothing, no trace whatsoever of this duo in the national medias! Not yet.

Her addresses are eagerly anticipated, brief, incisive. "One idea at a time, she says, but an idea and an atmosphere that remain, an idea and atmosphere that are eternal. You know, it is precisely the atmosphere that gives the idea perpetuity." In New York she works full time to further one of the Chinese Party and government's great ambitions which she sums up as follows: "To transform radically and replace the dominant political software that presents Western history as the unique reference, the central framework, the motor of everything that was, is and will be, to the exclusion of everything that was and will be."

"*That's over,*" she interjects when she is presented with the latest publications praising "a world that no longer exists and that will never again exist."

Other angles are used to assess her track record, evaluate her continuous ascent in the Party and the government, an ascent crowned when she is designated, in 2034, as the President of the Priorities Committee, a permanent committee within the political bureau of the Party. "One more step, notes a blogger, and Madame will be Secretary General of the Party and President of the Popular Republic of China. For once, we will then have to feminize everything: our language, our evaluation methods and the way we ask questions!"

As a Minister, she imposed a policy of consultation that contrasted sharply with the traditional practices of her ministry. She increased the commissions to which were invited top executives of public and private enterprises, top civil servants, representatives of the provinces and the large cities, scientists, and social participants of all kinds.

Commentators recall the big report, *China in the 21st Century*—the other little red book—that bears the signature of Wei Shu and made her known in the whole country. They note the similarity of method, the same insistence as concerns the relationship between theoretical analyses and proposals for their implementation that were given priority. They also emphasize, while using the necessary precautions, that the method allowed the minister, who was furthermore a member of the Permanent Committee of the Political Bureau of the Party, to occupy just about permanently a considerable mediatic space both in China and the world.

This jockeying for position was unprecedented, because normally members of the Political Bureau must balance their interventions in order to avoid crises at the highest level of the Party and the State; also, because it is indispensable, again to avoid crises, to take into consideration the interests and susceptibilities of the President of the Political Bureau. Now, since 2026, this President is Fang Zheng, Wei Shu's ex-father-in-law.

For two decades, the two have belonged to the same political movement and, within the Party, the Minister's action was decisive in Fang's election to the position of Secretary General and President of the Republic.

As soon as she took office as President, Wei Shu would offer an extremely favorable appraisal of the two mandates of her predecessor, "who is also the grandfather of my children."

Many of the subjects debated before the Priorities Committee of the Ministry for Economic Planning and Development that she directed excited public opinion. The list of these subjects was long: the project called "Phase 4" dealing with the economic, technological and social treatment of an essential resource that was becoming rare everywhere in the world—water—with the objective of zero loss as concerned the territorial and demographic giant that is China; the project called "Total Mobility" linking freedom of movement, internet mobility and personal mobility in this 100% digital country; two projects called "The Daigou of Greater Asia" based on interconnected investments between China, India and Japan in the ultimate generation of communication technologies. The ultimate generation, given the ability of computers to transform themselves and to move autonomously from one generation to another.

The aim of the first of these projects was to achieve "incalculable swiftness," sensitive anticipation of changes within the range of demands, the creation and sharing of adapted norms. The second strove to achieve incalculable depth, to substitute ocean depths for the present system so as to cool down cloud-like containers where hundred of billions of data were and would be stored; because there was also the project to make compulsory, as of January 1, 2034, the use of Chinese electronic currency in all private or public, national and international transactions with one or several Chinese partners.

In the many clandestine polls that circulated on the Web, the Minister's stature was becoming more and more impressive. As the *China*

Daily noted in a rare reference to these "doubtful practices imported from doubtful countries," the Minister always occupied "an honorable rank, almost the first, a dangerous zone if ever there was one, among political parties anywhere in the world."

The *Shifu* tells her continuously that she owes it to her beauty, her elegance, her rare talent as a communicator, to her well polished formulas that always make the headlines.

"What thoughtlessness, my friend, she retorts, really! You could have mentioned my handling of the economy without a crisis for nearly a full decade, my decisive judgments and the swiftness with which I put them into practice. And what about my conquest of New York!"

The *Shifu* then hugs her and says, in a low and neutral voice: "I withdraw these words at the request of the most beautiful, the most elegant, and the most convincing woman in China."

She pushes him aside gently and declares solemnly: "Comrade, as was said in our prehistory, I will never negotiate against you, since your mind is so twisted, twisted and beyond redemption."

"Star of the Party," the electronic newspaper *People* splashed on its headlines, in 2032, when announcing the ascent of Wei Shu to the Bureau of the Party's Permanent Committee. The Minister had burst out laughing: "Contradictions in terms!"

"No, no, retorts the *Shifu,* you have been a star and a great star since the presentation of your famous report. Tell me, what other woman can claim for herself such a continuous rise, more or less accelerated, certainly, but never interrupted, which is your trajectory in the Party?"

***

Everything had started in the family. The father and mother were both committed members of the Party. The history of their convictions differed, however.

The paternal grandmother had been a lacemaker at the imperial court, and her parents, civil servants of a floundering state, but were part of a long tradition of imperial administration that went back more than two thousand years.

Urbane, an inhabitant of the national capital, an expert on its rites, its certitudes and splendors, the father had left China after the Revolution, a member of the first cohort of Chinese students in foreign countries. He had discovered America and, as a good economist, he made a rigorous assessment of it: on the one hand, the accumulation of assets and, on the other, a corrosion which, in the medium term, would ruin it.

The future President of the Federation of Chinese Banks had come back home in the autumn of 1976, after the death of Mao and the arrest of the Gang of Four. A new era was going to begin with Deng Xiaoping's policy of openness. He had been among the very first teams entrusted with applying the Chinese brand of socialism, an economic policy that encouraged individual profit, performance bonuses, and the welcoming of foreign businesses. The regime's dogmas were getting water-logged. Everything was at risk, including hope, but at last it was emerging.

The Gang of Four was in jail, the Party had rallied behind Deng, the government had realigned itself, the specialized areas grew in number and the message was picked up in China, in the diaspora and in all the councils of the world's multinationals. The flow of foreign investments swelled way beyond any predictions. Encouraged by their governments, western multinationals delocalized their assembly lines and research laboratories. They installed large numbers of them in that very China offering abundant, docile and cheap manpower, in that China which was geared to becoming the biggest market in the world. *The flies will sense the honey and will set themselves down on it.*

Not only the urban areas, but also the rural areas were being metamorphosed. Some thought that Deng was the agent with a mandate from heaven.

Wei Shu conjures up those so unusual times to explain her invincible attachment to the Party. In her eyes, the latter is the only real lever which this country of one billion three hundred million inhabitants has at its disposal to ensure its growth, stability and the extension of its citizens' rights, especially their social and economic rights.

"You know, she repeats frequently to her visitors in written releases or in her speeches, I have seen, with my own eyes, the largest poorest country in the world become, within a generation, the biggest financial, commercial and economic power on the planet. Our Party has been the lever of this transformation unique in history. What an instrument it is, when it is held by fair and fertile minds like President Deng, whom my father advised during his whole presidency! In their times,

37

the emperors dealt with affairs of state behind a more or less opaque screen. The Party deals with affairs of state without a screen, in full view of millions of its compatriots."

***

On the maternal side, the paths had been very contrasted. In 1949, in the poor, abandoned, forgotten rural world, sorrowful memories prevailed. The memory of He Zuonen, Shu's grandmother, was filled with hardships piling up over time: the great droughts that had unleashed terrible battles between beasts and men for a few dried out twigs; treks of five kilometres, with fear in one's guts, to sell eggs at the market, near the little closed station, at the end of the road; the intense fevers that would kill you the way hurricanes razed villages, struck down animals and made forests bend without pity; bandits passing through who would take possession of anything that glittered, animals and sometimes even children; girls whose necks were twisted twice as soon as they were born and their bulging eyes that pursued you and installed you in a recurring nightmare. One also recalled the heavy rains that would drown the crops definitively, make the herds incoherent and liquify the dwellings of straw and cobs. To these were added the dramas of the Long March such as her father—a volunteer, then victim of this impossible yet executed project—had related them to her.

He Zuonen's memory was also filled with her experience as an intellectual in the throes of the Cultural Revolution: "I experienced brute fury, the destruction of my life's work, the terror of re-education demanded by the Party. I have never completely recovered from the hard labor light years away from the slightest human kindness. *In these lands gorged with blood not even the slightest hope can ever grow back again.* So many signs, so much misery, so much hardship!"

As for the maternal grandfather, he had celebrated in Beijing, in 1949, the proclamation of the new China.

"You naïve one! the grandmother said to her husband. He allowed himself to be seduced by a speech announcing the end of colonialism, the destruction of the former China that was corrupt, collaborationist and radically inegalitarian. He became a civil servant in the capital, set up his family there and let me pursue my passion for history. But the Cultural Revolution has annihilated my accomplishments and broken my spirit forever."

Jiang Sicong, the mother of Wei Shu, was the child of this singular couple. She would take up and complete her mother's historical work and win the respect and affection of her historian colleagues, both in her country and in the world.

In small strokes, through bedtime readings when she was little, discussions at mealtime when she was an adolescent, through her presence at her mother's book launches and lectures, the future President had ended up by sharing with her a keen interest in history and Chinese civilization.

From the lives of her grandmother and mother, Wei Shu would draw out two lasting lessons. Firstly, a sharp awareness of the grandeur of her country's history. Hence the horror she felt in the face of the appalling deviation from the purposes of the Party that was the Cultural Revolution. "While still in the early stages of my career, I strove to set up counterweights capable of blocking all possible drifts. As Secretary General of the Party, I would pursue this conviction arising from the history of the two women in my life, who made me see all the fury and all the sweetness of the world."

***

Wei Shu rarely talks about these environments which were so special in her personal life, except to recall the source of her convictions and her determination. She lived the first part of her life in a very politicized milieu made up of memories that were rich, active and contrasted, happy and unhappy at the same time.

Her father's life has been nourished by an exalting experience of political, economic and social renewal to which he had made a significant contribution culminating in the presidency of the Popular Bank of China. Her mother's life was torn apart between her formidable intellectual success as a world-famous historian and the physical and moral suffering of her mother, destroyed for all eternity.

Wei Shu's mind, comprising her hesitations and certitudes, was enriched by these experiences. Hence, undoubtedly, her absolute, but also very attentive loyalty towards the Party as well as the continuous attention she gives to what she calls, when bringing up the Universal Declaration of Human Rights, "the obligation to liberate the Chinese people from fear and want."

The analysts who have endeavored to understand Wei Shu's itinerary within the Party have all taken up this quotation attributed to her:

"My nomination to the Central Committee was prepared a long time beforehand ever since I gained control of the Youth League in 1997. For the first time, the *People's Daily* published my photo while identifying me arbitrarily, indeed falsely, with the conservative wing of the Party. As a result, I rose to the Central Committee. I was one of the two thousand five hundred delegates there, but I did not go unnoticed. I already had my clientele, the support of the youth and in the thousands, a title, speaking time, and the blue card that authorized me to take part in all the workshops.

"For the first time, I repeated incessantly during the same day: '*Da Jia Hao*, I am happy to be with you.'"

For the first time, I understood the true nature of the country, its demographic, ethnic, political and geographical dimensions, the weights of the provinces and the large cities, those of the army and the great scientific academies, those also of the Central Federal Power.

"For the first time, I could follow the deliberations that precede the choice of the two hundred members of the Central Committee and of the twenty-five members of its Political Bureau.

To move from the committee to the levels that count is like going up a ladder that gets lost in the fog and never being able to turn around or go down by even one rung. It means having faith in those who, below, are holding that ladder. They deserve for you to remember them forever, just like they, rest assured, remember you forever. This is what distinguishes the Chinese Communist Party from western political parties. The first is based on continuity: the seconds, on breakups.

"I figured out very early that at these high levels, it is better to remain silent than to talk without listeners both sympathetic and ready to spread your message. I also learned early that certain categories of Party members absolutely must be part of your alliance if you wish it to be a durable and winning one."

Studying Wei Shu's career and helped by algorithms devouring all her speeches, political pundits identified those famous categories that provided support to the future president and lit her way to the summit. They identified and described them.

The first of these categories concerns the presence of relay stations over the whole of the territory. She understands the soldiers who adopt you, who do not let you fall if you don't let them fall either, as well as the youth wing of the Party, that provides your proposals with the necessary energy, longevity and memory.

The second category concerns the presence of vertical networks which, from the base up to the highest levels, carry the proposals and share reactions to them, be they favorable or not. It comprises the scientists, economists, bankers, the various digital society operators, the high- ranking academics. All these people guarantee that your proposals will circulate up to the research institutes, the deliberative authorities, the reference publications and the important places of national management. Wei Shu reminded them, in one of her speeches, of their role in the creation of ChinaNet.at the end of the previous century.

What had to be done? Some maintained that the American Internet was overrated and that its technological offer would not go very far. Others insisted that our country not succumb to the American temptation, that it provide for itself instead an international network of digital links to fulfill its ambition of becoming the top internet system in the world through its geographic extension, the number of its members, and the quality and diversity of its applications.

Today, our system is used by more than 60% of the 6.5 billion internauts in the world, and 70% of the 35 billion objects are connected via ChinaNet. We owe this success to the Party, and the Party owes it to your vigilance, your competence and your perseverance.

Finally, the third category is that of the local, district, provincial and national decision-makers. Here is where political arbitration takes place, where budgetary allocations are decided and where common laws and rules are set up. In this category, alliances are often doubtful and ephemeral. Those that last lead to power, but the mortar can dry up and crumble rapidly. It is thus indispensable to constantly and in real time be aware of the alliances and oppositions, the failures and successes of political partners. Consequently, a kind of invisible and permanent spying is imperative.

Within the Party leadership and during her public speeches, Wei Shu ceaselessly reiterates the same theme that extolls both the advances of her country and those occurring elsewhere in the world.

I am my father's daughter and the daughter-in-law of President Fang. In these spheres of influence, they remember the famous statement of President Deng Xiaoping: "Put wind into the wind." This is what matters to me. To work so that our country brings to the world the fruits of its innumerable social, cultural, scientific and technological sites, and that it benefits from the same quality of activities carried out elsewhere in the world. I have joined forces and continue to do so, with the tendencies that are compatible with this vision. The party as a lever, our contribution to universal civilization as a source of pride, our recent accomplishments as proof of the fecundity of our form of government.

Wei Shu's political talent and charisma enabled her to draw out and strengthen a real cohesion between these categories. Her arrival and participation in the quinquennial meetings of the Party were choreographed with great care and modified according to the circumstances. Thus in 2012, 2017 and 2027, she kept a low profile, since the political space was fully occupied, first by the candidate Xi Jinping, in the first case, and in the second, the candidate Fang, her ex-father-in-law. On these occasions, she made herself less visible and less flamboyant. But essentially her program varied little.

She would meet with the members of the Communist Youth League and those of the Central Military Commission, a selection of governors and leaders of the large cities, she would dine with the members of the Scientific Commission and would receive hand-picked foreign delegations. At every plenary session of the Central Committee between 1997 and 2036, she would take the floor and state each time, once the references to the present situations were completed, the three major themes of her political vision: "The pride she felt on contemplating the unique contribution of China to universal civilization; the confidence generated when envisaging recent accomplishments, which have enabled the biggest poorest country in the world to become, within one generation, the foremost financial, commercial and economic power on the planet. Finally, the capability of the Party as a lever for these accomplishments when it is run by *fair and fertile minds.*"

Parallel to these intrinsically political activities, Wei Shu was pursuing a high-level government career.

National and international analysts held in high esteem the track record of the Minister for Economic Planning and Development. They acknowledged the success of China's new policy of foreign investments, which coincided with an impressive number of achievements in its negotiation with the World Trade Organization. Henceforth, the rules that would preside over trade would be constantly monitored, and the rule of "one country, one vote" would be abolished. That rule was replaced by a complex formula that favored countries with large populations, including obviously China, India, Indonesia, Nigeria, Egypt, Brazil, Ethiopia... As a somewhat captive clientele, the countries of Asia and Africa had given their constant support. Wei Shu had summarized the evolution of things in a definitive formula: "The citizens of the world are taking charge of the affairs of the world. Such will be the dominant economic and political trajectory during this first century of the new millennium.

She kept referring incessantly to her mission: *to radically transform and replace the dominant political software that allow western history to be the unique reference, the central plot, the motor of everything that was, is and will be.* She made it the centre of her schedules, her travels and all her speeches.

The plan was unfolding steadily. China had opened a large breach by withdrawing from the International Monetary Fund and the World Bank and by creating the Asian Bank that invested in infrastructures, and by fusing the Shanghai Association of Cooperation and the Secretariat of the New Silk Road to create an International Division of Norms and of International Cooperation. The OECD never recovered from it.

Wei Shu's role in these actions had been decisive. Clarity of objectives, rallying partners, rigorous timetables, swiftness in negotiations: this was the Wei Shu method at its best, without forgetting extreme politeness and implacable toughness.

In a famous lecture before the Berlin Chamber of Commerce, in the spring of 2035, the powerful Chinese Minister of the Economy had invited all the countries of the world to contribute to the establishment of new common institutions for the 21st century.

"Our conviction is unshakeable. Here, in the heart of Europe that has contributed so powerfully to the scientific and technological evolution of the world, these past centuries, I launch an appeal to those who share our assessment of the international system inherited from a bygone past. It is necessary to put an end to this body of obsolete institutions that handle texts which they alone can appreciate and understand, and even then! It is necessary to put an end to this body of institutions profoundly out of step with the realities and demands of our time. It is necessary to put an end to these apparatuses that depend on a few powers which, in the previous century, had the means to impose through force their interests on the nations of the world. As you know, these powers no longer have these means at their disposal.

"Our historic conception and the demands of our times coincide. It is necessary to give back to the nations of the world their intrinsic right to stake out for themselves the domains where they wish to fully exercise their sovereignty, the domains where they wish to share it, and to do this for whichever objectives, with whichever partners and for whichever time frame they choose. In this way will be recreated communities of debate and intervention which will have a meaning. In domains of world interest that they will have decided upon, they will be able to create vast ensembles that will better represent the needs of our time, notably in matters of international trade and technological development.

"We advocate free trade and we want to preserve it, make it fruitful for all. This signifies recognizing our abilities, which are great, and our limits, which are imperative. For this reason we have launched the New Silk Road, the 21st century version of it, known also under the name Belt and Road Initiative, or BRI, and have enshrined it in our Constitution. More than one hundred and fifteen countries have wished to participate in this unprecedented construction, in this vast network of land and sea routes, followed by material and immaterial realizations.

"China does not wish to dismantle the existing institutions. She is simply stating that they already are. Their members have backed away from them little by little and no longer answer the moving appeals of those who bear the responsibility of these large sick bodies. They are dying off and nobody is showing the slightest interest. As you know, it is the remoteness and indifference of the western powers far more than the supposed opposition of China that have created this vacuum. Clearly, the very people who thought up, developed and controlled these institutions in the name of principles of international liberalism have abandoned them after having used them to serve their interests. This crazy pendulum has shaken the community of nations hard; it has become languid, impoverished and without any perspective.

"China invites all the nations of the world, including the American nation, to this reinvention of international relationships. We believe that each nation possesses an indispensable fragment of the common sovereignty.

"Inspired by its realities and necessities, concerned about this common future, my country offers the community of nations more than a renovation of its apparatuses, an integral overhaul of the international system the need and demands for which are manifest. We know it and you know it: *Healthy shoots cannot come out of a sick bamboo tree.*

"It is necessary to put an end, a definitive end, to the powerful subversion that has perverted the modern and contemporary period, the negation of the experiences of others... these others who make up the majority in the world.

"In the long expanse of history, optimism, this philosophical and geographical posture that has sustained the American dream in the 20th century, is henceforth the privilege and the lever of the great Asian country, yesterday still ranked among the poorest on the planet and recognized, in 2035, as the foremost world economic power.

"During this last half-century, that fervor has transformed and allayed China's understanding of herself and of her historic and present role in world affairs. In addition, it has inspired a profound reinterpretation of the history of that great country, of the successive cycles in its coming together as a united nation. Entire chapters of its recent history have been erased, re-studied and corrected. Others have been glorified as so many stages that have changed its course, liberated hundreds of millions of people from the want and fear enclosing their lives.

"In the invisible universe where the essential plays out, this increase in Chinese optimism coincides with the expansion of American disillusionment. Finalized under Deng and reserved for the members of the Central Committee, the *Annual Appraisal of America* draws up a detailed inventory of the sociopsychological state of the United States.

"Published in 2020, one of these appraisals describes the 1990s as the last phase of the illusions of American political and military hyper-power in a world that had become *flat*. A phase also entertaining illusions about the digital age and its ability to make over the world alone. This same report describes the 2000s as the country's entrance into the age of doubt, a doubt affecting the military forces under the G.W. Bush administration, as a result of the difficulties encountered in Afghanistan and Iraq; a doubt that also affects the economy, because the long decline (2007-2012) caused by the sub-primes and the crash of autumn 2008 so damaged the American model. Something broke in a subtle way when it was understood that the money had been given to organizations responsible for the crisis rather than to its victims; when it was understood that jobs which had become scarce between 1990 and 2005 would certainly abound again, but under extreme conditions for the workers. The report describes the years between 2000 and 2010 as the age of disillusionment marked notably by the terrorist attacks of September 11, 2001, the military debacle in Iraq, in Afghanistan and Libya, the reassessment of digital power and the election of Donald Trump to the American presidency. This last event brought back to the foreground America's racial divisions. In addition, it led to the destabilisation of the Atlantic Alliance, Washington's abandoning of agreements for a free trade zone in the Asia-Pacific region and a free trade zone with the European Union. Finally, like an unleashed cascade, the most astonishing disengagements followed: withdrawal from the Paris Agreement on Climate and global warming; withdrawal from the Iranian Nuclear Agreement, from the Treaty on Medium Range Nuclear Weapons in Europe; withdrawal as well from several United Nations organs and programs, including the Council on Human Rights and, in the midst of the COVID-19 pandemic, the World Health Organization.

"Some assert that this deluge is the work of President Trump and could be reversed by his successor, Joe Biden. The dossier is more complex. Certainly, it bears the signature of Donald Trump, but also and indirectly of those who elected him and the representatives who, in Congress, enthusiastically supported this radical policy of disengagement. In short, America has broken ranks once. She could do it again.

"This ensemble of major events progressively fissured the ability of the Atlantic Zone to perceive itself as a coherent entity, capable of maintaining the institutions created after the Second World War and the security they were supposed to ensure. Outwardly, these institutions continue to exist, but the corrosion of the innermost components of the Occident House have affected them severely. Their internal order has sagged, leading to a cultural and ethical wobbling that prevents one from seeing the inner dysfunctions and correcting them.

"This ethical and ontological void has had the effect of concealing the immaterial flows of the world, of immobilizing the strength sustained by centuries of major advances in the continuous inclusion of all, and of allowing innumerable interest groups to draw closer to public power, to dominate it and to take possession of it as though it belonged to them. Any sharing of the wealth produced has thus become impossible.

"In short, in less than a half-century, The West has seen its four-time centenary economic domination of the world progressively collapse.

"In a first stage, its production capacity has been overtaken by Asia, to the point where the citizens of the Atlantic zone no longer had the means to buy what they produced themselves.

"In a second stage, the production capacity has entered a phase of qualified obsolescence. The present state of things has fissured the edifice of western democracies, that closely knit political, economic and social assemblage during a century marked by long cycles of growth and major crises, the continuous expansion of buying power, the installation of expensive systems of social redistribution and protection. More fragile than one imagined it to be, this assemblage has crumbled during the last two decades of the 20th century.

"Never in history had the conservatism and arrogance of State structures produced such a cataclysm, managing the unmanageable, pretending to reform systems already lifeless. So, the West, and Europe in particular, has entered a brutal social and worldwide disturbance.

"Chinese optimism is certainly fed by the recent economic, technological and social successes of the country. But it is also nourished by its reinsertion in the national return to ancient intellectual and cultural traditions.

"Inspired by the doctrine of Confucius, modern study of the Chinese mind-set expresses this intellectual and political reinvention of a history almost four thousand years old."

***

Wei Shu belongs to the leaders of the generation who wanted, conceived and made this reinvention succeed. Certain of her achievements bear her signature—with those of her friends and partners at the Chinese University of Political Science and Law, at the Central School of the Chinese Communist Party, at the Bureau of the President of the Popular Bank of China, at the Council of Affairs of State, and at the Political Bureau of the Party—and constitute as many stages in her exceptional political career. With several others, she is the artisan and the child of the Chinese dream that is offered to the world.

At a meeting of the regional party, in Shenzhen, Wei Shu had shared her understanding of what was happening:

"Political or cultural, political and cultural, our reinvention has followed multiple paths. It has found its protagonists in the youth wing, among the intellectuals, artists, creators and soldiers of the Party, supported by the historical allies, known or discreet, and the operators of Deng Xiaoping's philosophical and practical vision.

"It also found support in the circles of cultural creation. Videos, electronic games, documentaries, films, popular songs, festivals, symposiums, essays, novels, memoirs and chronicles show, each in its own genre, a fragment of what deserves to be unearthed, evaluated, enriched with the central elements of ancient Chinese history, which has apparently become central and indispensable again."

Wei Shu is inspired by the Shang dynasty that appeared three thousand years ago and reigned for five centuries. The unity of China and the emergence of a dominant Central State represent its major legacy. Moreover, the unification of the Chinese Empire is strengthened by the exercising of a strong central authority in charge of maintaining its territorial integrity. The idea and the reality of a strong central authority constitute the political legacy of that period. In the long run, this legacy has emerged as an evidence, a necessity, a precious gift to exploit and protect. The conviction took hold of a summons received from the heavens, a summons to guarantee the political, social and economic cohesion of the kingdom. Its successes are abundant: the unification of communities that had been scattered till then; technological advances as concerns the use of metals, notably bronze, the weaving of fibres, including silk, and the perfecting of pottery. Under the Shangs, urban life emerged, as attest their palatial cities, the installing of water pipes made of dried wood which changed forever the stability of communities. The mastery of water systems, the production of engravings and the use of ideographic writings enriched by thousands of characters changed forever the development of agriculture and the economy.

However opaque they may be, the ideographic inscriptions reveal the dimensions of the dialogue between the living and the dead, the living and nature, the questions asked and the answers expected. Delicate arabesques adorn the bronze vases and intertwine the secrets of these dialogues. Decorated with bold mazes, circles, squares and interlaces, the jade objects refer to mysteries surging forth from the original void "at the time when the uncreated occupied the whole of space." In that era, the figure of the phoenix came to the foreground, illustrating fear and the obscure part of being alive; the figure of the Dragons appeared as well, showing both the fertile and luminous parts of life.

Traversing the forty centuries of the history of China, and with it the duality of the Yin and the Yang, these opposing forces preside over the balance of the Universe and the life force.

These exploits are remarkable, just as was, in those ancient times, China's first geopolitical affirmation. Indeed, the control of the routes taken by the caravans towards Central Asia and the access to the resources of far-off lands that it allows represents a great premiere. It was made possible, another premiere, by the mastery of metals and the incorporation of iron in defense and offense arsenals.

More than two thousand years will have to elapse for events of such an importance to transform China so radically. If the revolution of three thousand years ago inaugurated the paradigm of the Chinese imperial system, the one in 1912 marked its definitive end.

Those who cannot encompass these two millenniums will never understand that contemporary China cannot be conceived without a strong central authority ensuring the identity and integrity of its national territory.

Wei Shu's China is the heiress of this first golden age of the great country. In her important national speeches, she never fails to refer to it. Her conviction is profound. It was in these very far-off times that were cemented in people's minds requirements, incessantly consolidated since then, pertaining to the unity of the territory between the southern sea and the plains dominated by the Mongols and opening onto Central Asia; pertaining as well to the exercising of the authority that wells from the central power instead and in place of local bodies; pertaining finally to the standardization of the multiple writing characters in a common system and to the unification of the codes, laws and measures that prevailed in the ancient kingdoms. To these advances were added a unified fiscal scheme and the recognition of minority rights. "History is sometimes faithful to what it was," Wei Shu likes to repeat.

"History is sometimes faithful to what it was. Our political and cultural DNA is ancient and solid, it has become enriched over the course of forty centuries and has benefited from the assets of humanity through the ages.

"How else to explain the fact that we have survived civilizations born along the Nile, the Tigris and the Indus? Only the civilization born along the Yellow River has lasted and will last for as far as one can foresee in the future.

"How else can one explain the permanence of our language? Anyone who can read our language today can read without too much difficulty a text written twenty centuries ago.

"I hold the answer to this bunch of questions from my mother, the most celebrated historian in my country in this century.

"China and its inhabitants carry within them the desire, the need, the tradition to solidly tie the past and the present, everything that is heavy in the past and everything that is unreal in the present, since it is not the past of anything, not yet. In the long expanse of our history, every reformist thrust, without exception, has inserted its roots far into the old and living Chinese memory. Yes, history is sometimes faithful to what it was."

***

In the narrative of this reinvention, certain disastrous episodes are nevertheless forgotten. One recalls especially the decree of the Qin kings, twenty-three centuries ago, targeting the destruction of works, sites, systems and leaders of everything that had preceded them. And the isolationist option of the Ming emperors in the 15th century after a moment of glory in the previous century, marked by the great census of 1393 and the introduction of the cadaster in the empire. This isolationist option had the notable effect of putting an end to the naval expeditions of Zheng He. The famous Eunuch with the rank of Admiral had navigated freely during thirty or so years on the western part of the Pacific Ocean and along the coasts of South-East Asia, from the Indeet of East Africa up to the coasts of Ethiopia. A tall stele set up in Sri Lanka and bearing an inscription in three languages has attested for a long time to the arrival of these Chinese visitors.

Published respectively in 1434, 1435 and 1451, the chronicles of Gong Zhe, Fei Xin and Ma Huan relate these voyages, describe the people encountered and the riches of the lands visited. Wei Shu is familiar with these accounts. One learns there that "jewel-filled boats," as those naval flotillas were designated then, also brought back the rarities of other countries, animals including ostriches and giraffes, spices, rare precious stones, some black slaves for domestic service and other necessities.

Certain physical imprints of the first golden age can be seen in modern China. In her improvisations, Wei Shu turns them to her advantage. She evokes then the network of roads that had sealed the empire's territorial unity and accelerated its economic development; the works undertaken to connect the fortifications of kingdoms henceforth part of an empire to be protected from nomads moving about in the Great North. A thousand years later, the Ming dynasty had made Beijing its capital, repulsed the Mongol armies and conquered the vast territories of the North. It had at that time resumed the "great project," had given the country its modern configuration, a kind of arabesque twelve thousand seven hundred kilometers in length and fixed its definitive boundaries from the Eastern Sea to the far-off frontiers of the Mongolian steppes.

"Centuries passed since that time. Generation after generation, we repeated that more than a million human lives were sacrificed to erect this stone ribbon, the only visible monument from space according to the accounts of marveling astronauts," as Wei Shu often recalls in her speeches.

Wei Shu venerates those ancient times, "those centuries of gestation that nourished and made us what we are." She "borrows" from the national museums some pieces that one can admire in her residences and places of work.

In the salons of her presidential suite at the People's Assembly, at the square of the Gate of Heavenly Peace, she exhibits a couple of stags poured into bronze of the Han era, a splendid horse's head in Tibetan jade and magnificent potteries from the same age. "This is what we were capable of doing in this country, about twenty centuries ago," she is accustomed to telling her guests.

In her Beijing dwelling, one can admire a bronze eagle of many evanescent colors. She shows it to all who visit her and describes it to them using the same terms: "This bird was born four millenniums ago in the mind of a Chinese foundry artist. He wanted this beauty and created it as you and I contemplate it forty centuries later. I am always moved when I look at him ready to take flight, with solid feet and a sharp eye. For me, it represents a pause in the upwards flight of my country, over the long extension of time.

Then, after a theatrical pause, she continues with obvious delight:

"Let me tell you where I found this treasure. In 2037, I was in London, on a state visit, and I asked to visit privately the Victoria and Albert Museum. Whole rooms were filled there with objects, sculpture, potteries, drawings, paintings and fabrics stolen from my country by the British, notably between 1856 and 1860, when they took control of the six most important Chinese ports, got hold of the capital, pillaged the Summer Palace before burning it. We hesitated and argued endlessly, as my African friends say. You know, the program is demanding, the schedules are set and security is already very tight. But I insisted "insistently", as my principal advisers say. I insisted "insistently."

51

"There I was, then, in the museum and in front of this bird which my father, as a student, had admired during a brief stopover in London, during his trip back home from America. He had photographed this beautiful bird, a photo I still have, that fascinated me and still does. During the state dinner, I asked that all the despoiled treasures be returned to us: I asked of the British Prime Minister at the time, Baha Khan, that he make a symbolic gesture and announce this return. And there you have it! The beautiful bird took the long flight in the presidential plane towards his nest, in my house! Since then, we have recovered two thirds of the treasures that our British friends had borrowed from us permanently, with a gun at our temple... in more diplomatic terms, that they had brutally borrowed from us."

These ancient objects, "fruits of those centuries of gestation that have nourished us and made us what we are," Wei Shu considers sacred.

The work of more than one hundred generations, China is now unified on a long-term basis, made secure, governed and having at its disposal a shared legal architecture. The whole is completed by having recourse to the Confucius doctrine, requisitioned, reinterpreted, and made to conform to the essential requirements of the great empire. Thus, like a vast spiritual alchemy, were fashioned the foundations of the culture, of the mentalities and the spirit of a China capable henceforth of viewing itself as a whole entity and conceiving itself as the foremost political power in the world.

***

The day after taking power, Wei Shu welcomes her personal guests at her large modern villa, near the National Museum of China.

Dressed in a royal blue sheath adorned with a cascade of Miaos necklaces in massive silver, the President, in her singular voice, begins to speak:

"I pay tribute to the successive generations who, over thousands of years, have made us what we are, and I celebrate the richness of the filiations that have created and strengthened the unity of our country from time immemorial. The solid network comprising our many experiences of these millenniums can be explained 'by the filial piousness and respect for the elders, these very roots of humanity,' in the words of Confucius.

"Dear friends, the responsibility of our generation is to share this heritage with the whole of humanity. Such are my resolve and my promise."

CHAPTER IV

THE EMPRESS AND THE PRESIDENT

PUBLISHED ONE WEEK AFTER THE ELECTION OF WEI SHU, *THE EMPRESS*, a little book by a certain May Fui, enjoys an immediate success in China and the world. On the cover, an astonishing photograph of the President Wei Shu. She appears there dressed and with a hair style like the dowager Empress Cixi, in the work of the Flemish painter Hubert Vos. The latter sojourned in Beijing in 1905, with the order to immortalize "the most seductive and powerful woman in the world, who has been reigning over China since 1861."

The dress, the color of light, is of silk with wide sleeves embroidered with turquoise cross-pieces. The hairstyle is smooth and crowned with a headdress of pearls and jade. The face is dominated by eyes of fire, as though magnetized by the immensity of what must be seen. Behind this austere personage, there are sequoia plants imported from the south of China for the gardens of the Summer Palace, two golden banners symbolizing imperial power, and obscured by a forest of young bamboos, the grandeur of a receding landscape, sumptuous and indistinct.

The intelligentsia and the political class speculate. Is it the product of an irreverent editor or the will of the President? A palace pamphlet or an enemy tract? An underhand blow or a mediatic coup?

The image invades China, printed on large posters, body vests, notebooks, tablets, cases, pennants, dishes and tumblers that national and foreign visitors are desperate to get their hands on. On the Web are offered squares of silk showing the famous cover, a woman of another era who captivates in her own.

The publicity agents take possession of the image. It is truncated to avoid prosecution. It is truncated, but it is used. In the evening, it emerges on hundreds of millions of screens that associate it with many products: from travel to perfume, from fashion to jewelry. The publicity agents multiply the offers which provide as many opportunities to share the images of Cixi and Shu. The official silence sustains the astonishment, the surprise, the rumours.

The short foreword of the little book links the destinies of these two women seated on the same throne, adorned with the same attributes, both beautiful, both distant from one another. May Fui's text fuses the two destinies, the words of one taken up by the other, the same phrases uttered by one and the other. Lives separated by time, but seemingly fused in their unfolding under the ambiguous pen of a writer who takes pleasure in inventing ephemeral lights to clarify thousands of mix-ups and as many mysteries.

The work is devoted to the Empress Cixi, to the long reign of that woman whose beauty was compared "to the purity of the purest jade."

A chamber maid in 1852, a concubine of the emperor Xianfeng in 1855 and dowager Empress in 1861, Cixi did not recoil from any means of reinforcing her authority and her control over the affairs of the empire: the purchase of the principal eunuchs; the placing in supervised residence of her adopted son and legitimate head of the State, the Emperor Guangzu; the execution of his principal counsellors held responsible for a plan, inspired by the Japanese model, to modernize China; her decisive support, then no less decisive condemnation of the peasants and workers brought together in the Boxer Revolt, from 1898 to 1901.

Through allusions, quotations, barely coded allegories, Wei Shu appears then fades away, in this light narrative where abound acts of cunning, nepotism, sex, oaths, assassinations and betrayals.

Cixi or Shu? The power of one or the power of the other? The ambiguity is permanent, the resemblances and differences, indisputable. Are they not, both of them, concubines or daughters-in-law of their predecessors? Do both of them not have, by their side, an obscure personage entrusted with performing good deeds and other acts, a eunuch or a Persian, unless it is the opposite? Did they not make secret alliances with the discrete, rich and powerful military oligarchy, the same, essentially, that existed a century and a half ago?

"Orchid" is the nickname that the two "Empresses" share. Around them, a retinue of eunuchs, their hands against their bodies, forced to be silent and compelled to hold the pipe of these two opium smokers. Overcome by the smoke of the imperial tobacco, Cixi's birds become crazy, let out cries that had never been heard, unpleasant ones for imperial ears. Enervated by such a cacophony, Cixi orders them to be killed.

What will happen, May Fui wonders, to Shu's ministers? Will they also be overcome by the opium odors? Will they have to ply the needle with their teeth when the cloth will be too thick, just like the women in the court of the dowager Empress?

In Cixi's time, whoever infringed the court rituals and the imperial whims had his right leg mutilated and his left one cut off. This amiable procedure applied also to those, male and female, who were responsible for maintaining the natural beauty of the woman with fish eyes and dragon pupils, but who failed!

The time for vanity is over. Shu, like Cixi, walks without moving her head and showers with rice water and infusions of shell pearls, round and brilliant. Are these stories based on fact or invented legends? Which of the two has her feet bound? Unless it is her mind?

Made up of nuances and complexities, the confusion is cunningly sustained in all things and especially as concerns the relationships of the two women politicians with the Occident.

The flight of the Empress Cixi from Beijing towards Xi'an, the result of the alliance of eight nations against China, and Wei Shu's mission at the United Nations intermingle there against a vague backdrop of corruption. Their respective return is presented as a clever strategy where get mixed dishonest compromises, intimate invitations, favors granted to certain counsellors—followed by their definitive disappearance—purchases of alliances and thirst for power. Without making it explicitly clear, the "Manchu Woman" and the "American one" are held personally responsible for the former and present obsolescence of Chinese institutions; their respective speeches about the "indispensable reforms" are presented as desperate, unscrupulous attempts to consolidate the stranglehold of the Palace on the country's wealth.

The end of the Empress Cixi's reign is likened to terror—summary executions of opponents, intellectuals and dissidents of all kinds. Consequently, the protests grow and finally put an end to three centuries of Manchu power. A sad end to the reign of the Qing Dynasty and to that "beauty comparable to the purity of the purest jade."

The pamphlet's conclusion is a blatant lie. If Cixi's contradictory but effective strategies enabled her to reign for a half-century, or one of the longest reigns in China's long history, they are the weapons of an era long-gone, fortunately long-gone.

Many yellowish photos of the dowager Empress Cixi and others, recent ones, of Wei Shu illustrate the work. Face to face, page after page, the two women appear linked by a common destiny, as though enveloped by an implacable passion shared in the continuity of history.

Who then is hiding under the pseudonym May Fui?

Adversaries of the President within the Party? Opponents of the regime? A writer or journalist paid by India or some other Soudan?

Who orchestrated the marketing of *The Empress* on a planetary scale? "The Book of the Year," according to the *Times* of London; "Essential and disquieting," according to *La Repubblica* of Rome; "An Enlightening Portrait," according to the *Japan Daily*. Millions of readers download the portrait of the century, and the text available in all the world's languages.

CHAPTER V

FANG ZHENG, THE PREDECESSOR

WITHOUT DENYING WEI SHU'S INDISPUTABLE QUALITIES, THE DYNASTIC appearance of the transition taking place, from the old president Fang to the divorced wife of his only son, is fodder for abundant commentaries in the chancelleries, ministries and medias. Camouflaged and veiled in many ways, the reference to nepotism is omnipresent, suggested, but rarely asserted with frankness.

Wei Shu replied slowly to a Japanese journalist who invoked this 'hypothesis" during her first press conference outside of her country and expressed astonishment on seeing a woman at the head of China. Her entourage knows that when she hastens slowly there will be fireworks. First a long silence, then a wide smile, this "kiss of death" feared just as much by her friends as her adversaries, she finally answers:

"I share the universal respect that my predecessor enjoys. In the assessment of statesmen of this century, he occupies and will occupy, over the long haul, one of the very first ranks.

"Under his authority and his wisdom, two of the thorniest problems in our long history have been definitively settled. China had four hundred and thirty million inhabitants in 1850, under the sign of the Dog, six hundred and fifty in 1950, under the sign of the Tiger, and one billion two hundred million in the year 2000, under the sign of the Dragon. Our population has doubled over the course of the first millennium, from sixty to one hundred million; it has multiplied by twelve in the second millennium to reach one billion three hundred million. This demographic framework is an essential fact for anyone who wants to understand our history, our form of government and our interests.

Over the long haul, our economy never disposed of a large enough base to reconcile these two movements. On this matter, our own statistics and those of international organizations, which are rarely favorable to China, converge.

"For centuries, our State was stumbling over this fracture separating our real abilities to produce and distribute wealth and the continuous growth of our population.

"Inaugurated in 1979, the policy of modern development produced a sustained growth for four decades. Then, we experienced the weakening of which you are aware. President Fang relaunched our economy through a policy of distribution unequaled in the history of humanity. Combined, these two policies have snatched from poverty hundreds of millions of my fellow-citizens, almost three quarters of the inhabitants of this country.

"This reconciliation hides another, which also has historical significance. Over the long haul, two Chinas have coexisted in a relation that was always difficult and often violent: a rural China that was a very large majority, enslaved, pillaged, in a permanently precarious state, and the other China, urban, armed and privileged.

"For the first time in its history, China is united, Chinese society and the Chinese State are reconciled and pacified. The successive empires have fallen, the result of peasant revolts: the Mongol one in the 13th and 14th centuries, undermined by the Red Turbans; the Ming one, afflicted by the Japanese expeditions in the 17th century; finally, the Qing one, inaugurated in 1644 and lasting until 1911, brutalized several times as a result of the famines of 1840, then during the Boxer Revolt. Further along in the past, three thousand years ago, the later Han dynasty did not survive the Yellow Turbans.

"Today, the China of the peasants is solidly reconciled with the nation. Today, the large regions of the North-East have caught up with the growth rate of the strongest areas in the country. Always sought and unrealized for three centuries, this very ancient aspiration is finally mastered. Such is, among others, President Fang's legacy of paramount importance, his incalculable contribution to the harmony prevailing in our country.

"In the same spirit, he worked successfully to smooth out social contrasts, to include in the sharing of wealth those who, for different reasons, were excluded from it. It is the very spirit of our permanent revolution that demanded these redresses.

"Finally, since it is necessary to choose, let me recall his urban policy, bold in all of its measures. Our results are spectacular and the envy of the world. One thousand Chinese cities have more than a million inhabitants. China has invested massively in the environmental, social and cultural dimensions of its cities.

"Having lived abroad and visited the world's cities, I do not hesitate to assert that our urban civilization is the most advanced in this 'millennium of the cities.'

"I will say assuredly after many others that his presidency makes one think of the golden age of our country, between the middle of the 17th century and the middle of the following one.

"Finally, as you know, President Fang is also the grandfather of my two children. They have had this good fortune, this privilege. He is a true *Sherpa* for each one of them. You can see how happy and moved I am. With others, but in a constant manner, I have worked by his side in the different functions that were his in the Party or the government. Under his authority, I have represented my country at numerous international conferences, then at the United Nations. Before just as after this mission, I have served as the Minister for Economic Planning and Development, responsible for investments.

"These links and experiences are very dear to me. They, however, have nothing to do with my election. Ambitions other than mine have manifested themselves. Finally, I have benefited from the choice of the majority of the members and executives of our Party. Believe me, like the spider and the ant, I myself have been weaving the strand and imprinting my traces for a long time.

"As concerns your astonishment about my gender, I leave you with this infatuation for realities of another era. I will say, however, that on numerous occasions in our history, contrary to yours, women, and many more than you can imagine, have held the top job in my country. I am thinking, among so many others, of Song Qingling, a stateswoman, Vice-President of the popular government in 1949 and, afterwards, head of our State. I also recall Li Zhen, the first woman General of our army, during the 1950s."

Here was terrific material for the satire sheets and the popular blogs, for the columnists who turned this woman into their unique subject of interest; then for all the others who constantly gather clusters of fantasies.

Now, fourteen centuries later, you have the return of the Tangs, the fantasy of Yang Guifei, the famous concubine of the Emperor

Tang Xuangong. After a brief sojourn in a Buddhist monastery, the beautiful courtesan had come back to the new Emperor. The latter's impotence and the birth of a son had catapulted her for a long time to the supreme office.

Will she be of the Tang lineage, the scribes wonder? Will she be of the Ming lineage, in the image of the Empress Yang Guifei, the daughter-in-law then the wife of Tang Xuanzong, whom the latter, dazzled by her beauty, had snatched from his son, the heir apparent!

The Emperor is no longer! Long live the Empress! Remarkable continuity of a clan, of its interests and privileges. The caricaturists malevolently repeat the simple phrase: "He is the grandfather of my two children."

The Fang and Shu families had been intimately associated for decades. Both came from the Fularji district, in the province of Heilongjiang, in the North-East, the heart of Chinese heavy industry, but their lasting ties only developed later. They were consolidated in America, during the 1970s. Students at the celebrated Princeton University, President Fang and Wei Shu's father had become friends and had discovered together "the decadent and dazzling America."

America had appeared decadent to them, because the cycles of internal and external violence that were running through it at the time was so undermining its claim of serving as a model; because its political system also seemed so overwhelmed, and its democratic ideal so imploded. The trauma of the assassinations of the pastor Martin Luther King Jr., in Memphis, and of Robert Kennedy, in Los Angeles, hovered then over a society split apart by the riots of the black American nation, the noisy and often violent student agitation, and the massive and continuous demonstrations by all against the war in Vietnam.

Abandoned in 1968 by Lyndon B. Johnson, power was in the hands of Richard Nixon, a power conquered at the end of an electoral campaign dominated by three supporters of an outmoded order: Richard Nixon, the ghost of the 1950s; Hubert Humphrey, the outgoing Vice-President, and George Wallace, the white supremacist Governor of Alabama.

Incredulous and stupefied, the two students had observed the cities that were burning, the devastated campuses, the public property destroyed and the ongoing battle between the White House and Congress. Also, the inability of the system to recover its power in order to make decisions and respond to the immense demand for equality and justice that was feeding the national crises of the time.

From their vantage point in the United States, they had heard the loud clamor that was rumbling in the world's capitals, a clamor of the multitudes condemning the war run by the Americans in far-off Southeast Asia, the American war in Vietnam, at the border of their own country.

If America was burning on its own territory, it was also burning in the minds and hearts of its opponents in Madrid, London, Berlin, Moscow, Montreal, Rome, Tokyo, Cairo, Mexico, New Delhi and in so many other cities still. For the Chinese students as well as for a large number of people, America had become a land of distress, the area of the world where evil had chosen its dwelling.

This immense drama bearing fire and blood could be seen day after day on the television screens in the university residences of the two Chinese students. Vietnamese bodies blown up; processions of coffins carrying *boys* by the hundreds on the runways of military airports; Vietnamese villages burned by napalm along with everything that was alive there, humans, animals, plants within a five hundred metre radius; neighborhoods of American cities set on fire, pillaged, ruined because they were assaulted by the police; flags with the fifty stars and the effigies of Nixon and Johnson that were burning in large public places, from Times Square to Michigan Avenue, from Cambridge to the Stanford campus, among dozens and dozens of others.

The Chinese friends had listened to the never-ending discussions of the elected officials, the experts, the military people and the Black leaders, all incapable of breaking the infernal circle which, from Washington and Saigon, was destroying everything that approached it, men, minds and gods.

They had also read the cult works of the time. *An American Dream,* by the Great Norman Mailer, had shaken them up. Starting with the story of a murder in New York falsified as a suicide, Mailer conjured up the American pandemics: drugs, alcohol, racism, unleashed sexuality, corruption, poverty... Were the country and society condemned to this descent into hell as evoked by that author? No, answered Martin Luther King. But the great speeches made by the Black pastor, including *I Have a Dream*, read and commented on by the Chinese students, had been immediately contradicted in their essence following the sordid assassination of their author.

America had also appeared as "dazzling" to them. Despite the storm, it still dominated the world geopolitical scene and showed itself capable of bold initiatives.

If the war in Vietnam drew much of the attention, the other war, called the Cold War, of which the first was a fragment, was determining the world's future. And America was clearly dominating that one. The two friends found it difficult to support the Kremlin. But they played the loyalty game and condemned America, its subterfuges, its contradictions, its brigades at work in the world.

Washington had conducted two secret negotiations, one with the representatives of the North Vietnam government, in Paris, the other with the representatives of the Chinese government, in Warsaw.

The famous triangular diplomacy decided upon by Nixon had produced spectacular results in 1972, five years before Wei Shu's birth. The American President's trip to Beijing had put an end to an isolation policy of China at the end of a week that had "changed the world."

The first Nixon, the one of the 1950s and 1960s, considered the Chinese leaders "international criminals." The second Nixon, the 1970s version, appeared with Mao Zedong, celebrated the rigor and cordiality of Zhou Enlai, signed the Shanghai Declaration that made convergent "our different ways of reaching the same goal."

When he returned to Washington, Nixon uttered a simple statement which, in itself, expressed the profound change in the relationships between the United States and China: "What impressed me on the occasion of this trip and in my conversations with the Chinese leaders, is their deep conviction and their unswerving commitment to their system of government. That is their right, as is the right of all countries to choose the kind of government that they want."

Of all the arguments put forward by the CIA, the Defense Department and many allied countries against this trip to China by the American President, the fear, indeed the certitude of a hardening of the Soviet Union, occupied the foreground.

That fear had been confirmed by many warnings formulated by the leaders of the USSR. The *bluff* of the century, according to Nixon, convinced that the new relationship of their country with China would weaken "the senile Tsars" of the Kremlin. The immediate history proved him right. In that very year of 1972, Washington and Moscow signed the treaty limiting strategic armaments and launched s special cooperation program crowned by the rendezvous between *Apollo* and *Soyuz* in space in 1975.

These formidable American accomplishments also occupied the thoughts and discussions of Fang Zheng and his comrade Wei. But their judgment had been quietly strengthened. Fang had put his cards on the table in front of his father: "Don't be worried, I will return home despite the new difficulties. My future is not in this country where everything is going to the dogs. My future is by your side, in the service of China."

Unlike many of their Chinese comrades studying abroad, Fang Zheng and Wei Mao had returned to China in 1976, the very year of Mao Zedong's death, after a brief stopover in London. Certainly, the work of the Great Helmsman was still revered and the promises formulated in 1949, from the height of the Tian'anmen Gate, still constituted the dogma of reference. But Mao Zedong's long reign had also left an abundance of painful marks.

At the top of the list, there was the appalling manipulation of the Hundred Flowers, in 1957, which had liberated speech only to better stigmatize those who had availed themselves of it freely, at the invitation of the most important of the Chinese. What followed afterwards was the monumental drama of the Great Leap Forward, launched in 1958 for the purpose of equaling, indeed surpassing the economy of the West, and which had produced one of the greatest shortages in history and caused millions of deaths. Eight years later, in 1966, in opposition to the Soviet revisionists, and having become "the only trustee of Marxist orthodoxy," China had known its third monumental tragedy under Mao's leadership: the Great Proletarian Cultural Revolution.

The country to which Fang Zheng and Wei Mao returned was devastated, its mythology exhausted, its messianism degraded, without any substance or interest. This drama was also an opportunity, because the need for reconstruction can be such a vector for innovation and modernity. Everything seemed outdated in the large cities: the television halls for the largest number of people, the state stores with limited provisions, the loudspeakers that blared out warlike music and imperative political messages in the public squares, the strange noise of bicycles, so different in Chinese cities from that of automobiles in American ones, also, the odors, and then the blue uniform of China, that would prevail for some time yet. All that would change rapidly, from music to clothes, from state stores to free enterprise dealers, from public companies to private ones, from insecure jobs to technological ones and from unobtainable services to a service economy.

Another important change: without any announcement and fuss, under lock for more than a quarter of a century, the doors of Buddhist temples would open and many would pass through them.

63

Fang Zheng had chosen the political path and supported the profound reforms that Deng Xiaoping proposed. Wei Mao had chosen the economic path and joined the very first team entrusted with the responsibility of defining the conditions for direct foreign investment in China. The two former Princeton students had nevertheless maintained the relationship that had united them since "their exile among the Yankees."

The daughter of one would marry the son of the other, and the two friends would mount all the rungs in their respective spheres while combining their interests and networks. One would accede to the top political office in the country; the other, to the presidency of the Federation of Chinese Banks.

The alliance between the two clans would never flag. It would contribute to their spectacular parallel ascent. *Once gum has bonded with shellac, who could ever succeed in separating them?*

These fervent guardians of the political orthodoxy of the Popular Republic had witnessed and participated in the penetration of foreign economic models, resources and systems within their country. They had belonged to the teams that were doing the sifting: high strategy, smart diplomacy, transformation of the referents in public power, work done on the language relating to the Party, to the population, to regional and international institutions, to the heads of large businesses and to international investors.

***

Wei Shu grew up during "this blessed time" which profited from the shifting of the world's wealth from the West towards the East and benefited from the most important technological transfer in the history of humanity, a shifting and transfer that favored China.

In the large family house in the Wangling neighborhood, in the north-east of Beijing, the young girl witnessed, in the spacious garden, in the library and during meals, passionate debates and ardent pleas. She observed the constant comings and goings of personages in dark suits and carrying briefcases stamped with the red star. The ambassadors of India, of Brazil, of the USSR, of the United States, of Iran would come, as would King Sihanouk and Queen Monique, Indira Gandhi, Ibrahim Babangida, the President of Nigeria, Akihito, the heir apparent of Japan, Kim Il-Sung, President of North Korea, and, on several occasions, Lee Kuan Yew, the founder and first leader of Singapore.

The President sometimes evokes one of those very unusual dinners in these words:

"The house was filled with military people, photographers and foreigners who were all very kind to me and my sister Ma. Our dressmaker had made for us long dresses of bright yellow with large blue belts. We looked like false twins, an assessment that has pursued us all our lives. As a rare occurrence, that evening, we were allowed to remain in the large hall until the guests departed.

"The house was beautiful, lit up, decorated with flowers. The quartermaster, his wife and the officers occupied the large entrance. My father was waiting near the main door. He went out and returned accompanied by Lee Kuan Yew. I found him handsome, tall, elegant, speaking a lot and in a loud voice. "Stop, you're exaggerating," Ma told me.

"There they were, they seemed happy to be together. Suddenly, the hustle and bustle grew, men dressed in grey entered and formed what appeared to be a watertight guard of honor. One of them was moving about, listening to messages through his earphones. This apparent leader drew closer to my father and spoke to him discreetly. At that moment, the latter rushed towards the exit to welcome another guest, President Deng Xiaoping. He was a smiling, kindly little man. He greeted everyone, with his head inclined downwards. He was called at the time "the little giant producer of miracles."

"What happened, that night, in the dining room, between these two men and my father? What did they say to one another? What strategy did they finalize in that blessed era when the economic circumstances were favorable? As for me, I have a vivid memory of the evening, the memory of Deng Xiaoping's departure. He passed quickly in the large entrance hall, then came back towards us. He kindly put his hand on my sister's head and said: "Good luck at school. Do well and that will take you far in life. China will need you."

"What then had happened? The commentators at the time were speculating, but nothing filtered through from the participants or their entourages. It was as though the dinner had never taken place.

"Years later, in one of his writings, Deng Xiaoping described "a secret dinner" where "were discussed and set up the foundations of the operation Qin Shi, which will change international relations and modify the organization of the world." My father confirmed to me later that it was indeed that dinner offered in our house on the evening when my sister and I wore our bright yellow dresses with large blue belts."

***

Fang Zheng was entrusted with the task of setting up a plan aiming for the eventual penetration of powerful Chinese conglomerates in the world. He was to devise it in close cooperation with Wei Mao, the economist.

Between them, they had banked on the expansion of the conglomerates, that needed to be complemented by initiatives of another nature. Thus, after seasons of deliberations within the Party, would be engendered the network of the Confucius Centres and, later, the colossal project of the New Silk Road.

At the large family table, Wei Shu witnessed those unending discussions, the spectacle of glasses raised to celebrate some Chinese victory or other at the United Nations, in Geneva, Sao Paulo, Nairobi or Rabat, those new partnerships with some or other part of the world. She would hear sentences like: "We still need a quarter of a century"; "Thank you Germany, our only real ally in Europe"; "The American President must learn mandarin"; "Dallas is for sale, but alas, there are no buyers!"

In one domain after another, in one negotiation after another, China's economic and commercial presence grew stronger, her norms became the dominant ones and, with them, commercial practices transformed themselves in accordance with her economic and geopolitical interests.

Fang Zheng had been the skillful, discreet and effective artisan of these spectacular advances. He had been able to count on his friend, the powerful President of the Federation of Chinese Banks. His national and international reputation had grown. He was not seen much and was not heard much. He had climbed the rungs, one by one, had become Vice-Prime Minister, Secretary of the Central Committee, then member of the Political Bureau of the Party and, finally, President of the Popular Republic of China.

***

Wei Shu belongs to the closed circle of those who have been able to observe at close range China's liberation from a financial, economic and commercial isolation that had enclosed it for about a half-century. She belongs to the intimate world of the Fang clan where the strategies of this liberation had been discussed and planned on a daily basis, where the advances had been assessed, where the obstacles had been identified, where the assets had been recorded.

This unique situation is the durable effect of the link uniting the two families since the American sojourn of their heads. For about thirty years, their political and professional, personal and familial intimacy has remained constant and solid.

Festival of Spring on the first day of the lunar year, Festival of Pure Light, Festival of the Dragon Boats, Festival of the Moon, visits, vacations, birthdays, deaths…the memories of the two families, their joys, networks, defeats and successes were joined. Also, their photo albums which would be placed under seal after the election of Wei Shu.

This interconnected membership would be enriched by the marriage, in 2004, of the Fang son, Fang Jie and the Wei daughter, Wei Shu. The newlyweds had known one another since their earliest childhood.

The wedding celebration would last a good week, just like the festival that had brought Jie and Shu together in Shanghai, in 2000, to commemorate the linking of millenniums.

On that night, nearly one thousand five hundred drones had directed a beam of light towards outer space and had conjured up, in that far-off distance suddenly so close, a human silhouette dominating the terrestrial one. From all horizons, from Peru to Nepal, from Poland to Togo, from Vanuatu to Haiti and elsewhere in the world, billions had recognized themselves in that persona gliding in infinity.

Or there was also the great baroque celebration that had taken place when Wei Shu was twenty-six and had just finished her M.A. degree at the Central School of the Party. On the evening of the graduation ceremony, every male and female student had sat down on an artificial throne to hear their colleagues praise them on the occasion of a well-spiced drunken binge.

Elegantly attired in a white pearl outfit signed by a future famous name in Chinese haute couture, Wei Shu had taken her place on the throne. Her comrades disguised as Americans had taken turns speaking and justifying their choice, for or against Shu's election at the *Miss America Contest,* the third millennium vintage of the Chinese Communist Party's Central School.

She had, of course, been elected in the first round. Confetti fell from the sky, from a ceiling where the famous fifty stars had been drawn. American beer was served as well as popcorn imported from San Francisco and cheese cakes that were a bit heavy, but, said her friend Huamei, produced by a 3D printer in Chicago. She was crowned, wrapped up in a wide "American blue cape and given a rather small bouquet of dried flowers before being handed the microphone.

"Dear friends of all sexes, and the others, I have observed you very attentively. I have found you worthless, superbly worthless. By going to vote with the music of a singer who was undoubtedly a Slovak or Texan from the previous century, you looked like an animal herd coming out of the jungle to move on, night after nigh, to the same pond. I do not thank you. I do not congratulate you. I do not envy you, you poor things.

"You voted even though the outcome was self-evident. No one among you noticed this and you want to govern China and the world! How you disappoint me!"

"Who can really claim to possess, as I do, all the physical and intellectuals ace cards required to exert a function of this importance? I will be an exemplary *Miss America*, domineering, without scruples and will serve, at all times, Beijing's interests.

"With my right hand, I will draw a square in time and, with my left, a circle in space. My laser beam will try to penetrate your opaque minds. Here you are all confounded! There is not any small crown nor any small victory if one considers that they all contribute to reaching the ultimate goal, namely, to hoist oneself up to the first rank in the government of our country."

The speech had been a bit too long, but brilliant and hilarious. The orator had moved effortlessly in the labyrinths she had created and made them collapse in loud, sonorous laughter or in profound silence. They lose her trace, then rediscover it.

"Your speeches were rather painful to listen to, except for Fang Jie's. A Chinese or future Chinese wife knows where her interests lie. I am telling Jie that, except for the first, second and last part of his speech, he was brilliant, more brilliant than all of you put together. It is true that one does not really know how swiftly a horse can run when he runs alone."

***

Jie and Wei shared the same history both social and familial as well as political and ideological. They had in common reflexes, references, prejudices, anxieties, assessments of social events. They were part of the new Chinese aristocracy which, progressively, was replacing the family lineages born with the founding of the Popular Republic of China in 1949. It appeared that they were turning the pages of the same catalogue, Jie to conform to it, Wei Shu out of "social conformism," which was the equivalent of a well disguised disinterest. She was on the verge of a career that would combine "foreign economics and politics, strategic analysis and political rootedness." He was dreaming of a career as a manager of collections of historical artifacts, as a director of teams responsible for "healing the wounds caused by the Cultural Revolution," according to his words. He would realize his dream when he became, in 2028, the youngest director of the National Museum of China. She was dreaming of a political career that would reach an important conclusion when she was designated, in 2034, as President of the Priorities Committee, the Permanent Committee of the Party's Political Bureau. "One more step, a blogger had noted, and Madame will be the Secretary General of the Party and the President of the Popular Republic of China. When that happens, we will have to put everything in the feminine mode!"

Jie was a disciple of the Annals School that Shu's mother also venerated. In a burst of pseudo-sincerity that cost him a string of reproaches, he had let slip during an important dinner at his father's home: "Only a French scholarship for a training course at the Louvre School could postpone the date of my marriage." Shu had contented herself with saying loud and clear: "Our marriage." The poor guy would regret all his life "this infidelity," according to Shu, "this thoughtless word," according to Jie. One did not take, with impunity, a casual attitude towards the Wei girl's schedule, either at that moment or ever.

After their marriage, the lovers had set out for Gunag'an, in the province of Sichuan. They had visited there the museum dedicated to Deng Xiaoping, constructed next to his modest place of birth. They had also admired the valley of the Laba river and the beauties of the old city of Shangli. Finally, they had bottle fed the baby pandas at the famous sanctuary in Bifengxia. Wei had written to a friend:

Love, politics and nature, in the order you can imagine. We'll see what love brings. We know that the policy of our chief architect has multiplied by 44 the size of our economy and that nature, in itself, has been dazzling us since its very beginnings.

My father, who has worked for Deng, told me one day that the latter enjoyed love, politics and nature. I, too, enjoy this trilogy… but you will have to imagine in which order!

After their children's amorous parenthesis, the two fathers, Fang Zheng and Wei Mao, found themselves together again at the same discussion tables, both of them levers of the vast operation to ensure the entrance into the world market of the powerful Chinese conglomerates. Here were combined the reciprocal fruitfulness of the State's organizational abilities and the resources of the private sector.

Fang Sheng also used the full weight of his authority to accelerate the reform of the judiciary system. "Urgency, Urgency," he pleaded, inasmuch as so many events of the last quarter century called for such a reform, especially as a result of the general use of algorithms for the identification, the evaluation and the conduct of individuals, limited communities, the nation and the world. As a result, also, of recent environmental catastrophes, including the partial destruction of Amsterdam, of the Cape and the Grand-Lahou, a submerged city on the West African coast, and the increase in the number of pandemics since the COVID-19 outbreak of the 2020s. These events had brutally raised the question of the responsibility of all humanity and of all human beings, responsibility being the inseparable complement of rights. The system at that time had become obsolete and human survival demanded norms combining rights and responsibilities.

President Fang had also got started the reappraisal of the country's political system. It was out of the question to challenge the Chinese model, that composite of state control and free enterprise, or the proclaimed continuity of the one Party "with several branches," according to the expression used again and again by the President. Nevertheless, Fang Zheng had freed intellectual initiative, set up a complex architecture to guarantee on all levels an almost permanent consultation with the organizations of civil society that now enjoyed real leeway. This regime of rights and responsibilities would have to rely on an independent judicial system.

Finally, at the very end of his mandate, President Fang had proposed two major reforms: the male-female parity, on all levels, in the organs of the political and economic administration of the country and the party, and the abolition of the death penalty.

A Confucian and a liberal, Fang Zheng had carried out this body of reforms while endeavoring, as he said, "to master the tides." This excerpt was quoted from his latest work:

I do not belong to that race of politicians who blame the people and I am not a navigator who is in revolt against the sea.

Authority and autonomy, hierarchy and initiatives, stability and innovations, rights and responsibilities must be combined. The study of the modern Chinese mind-set comes at this price. It corresponds both to the needs of our time and the lessons arising from a history several thousand years old. It embodies this thirst for harmony that is omnipresent in the Chinese philosophic tradition and its absence, also omnipresent, in the long political history of our country.

Man carried an ambition inversely proportional to his rather modest stature: to extend to the world the new synthesis at work in China.

Borrowed from the most ancient writing of Chinese alchemy and chosen with great care, his maxim, *Putting wind into the wind*, translated his determination to propose, to convince and to act.

To his adversaries, partisans of small steps, frightened at the thought that the world system might collapse, he answered without blinking: "The spectre of the void is not in movement, but rather in the present stagnation." Referring to the ancient empires, those of the Hans and the Songs who lifted Chinese civilization up to undeniable peaks, the old President pleaded for boldness and constancy, convinced that an exceptional set of circumstances was offering itself to China which had become again the foremost world economy.

When dealing with the authorities of the regime and in public forums, Fang Zheng tirelessly repeated his central theses.

"From time immemorial China has been the victim of successive waves of conquerors and subjected to value systems imposed on her by force. She fought them, absorbed them, and revitalized them in certain cases. Tartars at the end of the Han dynasty at the beginning of the first millennium; Tibetans in the 8th century; Mongols in the 12th century at the end of the Song dynasty; Europeans, Russians and Japanese from the 17th till the 20th centuries, under Ming rule.

"Over the long haul, Buddhism has combined with the thinking of Confucius and the Taoist ancestral practices. The western system and the Japanese experience have been attractive but have remained outside of our civilization until the second half of the 20th century, when they have, following our own decisions, crossed over the Great Wall. During this same century, Marxism-Leninism has dominated our political system. It still constitutes today the vertebral column of our society and our State. It has been said, and rightly so, that Buddhism far more than China was transformed following its intrusion in Chinese civilization. This truth is also self-evident in the case of Marxism-Leninism and the western system.

"What then is the intangible substratum which this body of aggressions, conquests, dominations and influences was unable to alter within us? Subjected to less frequent and less redoubtable traumas, other civilizations and other powers have collapsed or have broken up into several minor entities.

"The permanence of China is an indisputable fact, an incomparable fact. The Han heritage has crossed the millenniums. We have pulled our territory together and unified our language. The Ascendancy of our State, the vigor of our public administration and our jurisprudential law system have endured even if they have been damaged by very powerful external forces. It was also during that period that the famous Silk Road, the trade route between China and Iran, was created, and that China discovered Europe.

"Struck by internal convulsions of great consequence, China has always re-emerged from those times of desolation and devastation thanks to her inalienable nature. Despite her unequalled upheavals and the covetousness of the many towards her through all the stages of her long history, China has endured for thousands of years. Other civilizations that were her contemporaries two or three millenniums ago have slid into non-being.

"After more than a hundred or so generations, ours has the obligation to protect, reinforce and exalt this intangible inheritance.

"What then are the next stages for China? What must she do with this ability to create that has become the foremost in the world?"

In his large garden, in the western suburb of Beijing, the old President was cultivating orchids and the eternal history of China, his hands soiled by what is perishable, his mind absorbed by the histories of his people, the one already accomplished, and the one to unfold in the future. On the one hand, the needs created by circumstances, and on the other, the exigencies of the long haul, between the material and carnal reality of China and that immaterial witness moving from generation to generation for nearly four thousand years.

***

Wei Shu is impressed by this wise old man. He is the President of his country and of the Party, the head of the government. He is also her ex-father-in-law, the grandfather of her two children. As she will say later, she is "seated at all the tables where President Fang happens to be, the family table, the ministerial table and the international tables." She will say one day about the wise old man whom she admires, that "he had a powerful way of being modest, which is to say, a modest way of being powerful."

CHAPTER VI

CONFUCIUS AND WEI SHU

TWENTY-FIVE CENTURIES HAVE ELAPSED BETWEEN THE DEATH OF Confucius and the election of Wei Shu. From the distance of these millenniums, the resemblances between the doctrine of the civil servant of the Zou State during the time of the Zhou dynasty and Wei Shu's conception of human nature, of the organization of society and of the administration of the world, are startling. More than a thousand times, the President has proclaimed her adherence to the Confucian philosophy, "for China and for humanity."

From her childhood onwards, the President has been finding sustenance in the thinking of Confucius. In a little salon of the large family home, near the Forbidden City, is preserved the altar of the ancestors with its tablets that go back to 1826. There, too, in an invisible hiding place, can be found two forbidden photos, one of the Dowager with the true love of her life, the head of her eunuchs, and a photo of Puyi, the adolescent who succeeded her and became the last Emperor of China. One sees him on the day of his abdication, in 1912, at the Palace of Celestial Purity, surrounded by all the luxuries possible, at the very moment when the several thousand years old Chinese imperial system died out.

Wei Shu's tutors had chosen this little salon to have her memorize the master's conversations, the way Muslims do with the text of the Coran. They also taught her the effects of the master's doctrine on the nation's history and the destiny of the successive dynasties that had held power.

The division was clear between the dynasties that conformed to the doctrine and enjoyed as a result indisputable prosperity, and all the other ones.

In the first category were the Hans at the beginning of the first millennium; the Tangs between the 8th and 10th centuries; the Songs until the end of the 13th century, and finally the Mings until the middle of the 17th century. These dynasties were not without flaws, but they succeeded for the most part. They had in common the fact that they had placed the philosophy of Confucius in the topmost ranks of their references and had regressed when they drew away from it.

In the second category were situated the regime of the Three Kingdoms in the 5th century, then that of the Manchus, from the middle of the 17th century till the beginning of the 20th. If the latter seemed to accord a genuine importance to the Confucius doctrine, it was much more to bring the Hans and the Mandarins of the former regime over to their side rather than out of respect and a profound adherence to a form of thought that defined the Chinese mind-set. On the contrary, their policy was the exact contradiction of it.

From these teachings emerged a vision of Chinese history and a major acknowledgement: fidelity to the thinking of Confucius had guaranteed the stability, the unity and the prosperity of the nation. Here was thinking nuanced by the necessities of the time at the different stages of the country's history.

Such had been the first encounters between Confucius and this frail and determined adolescent, living next to a very great historian, her mother, and in family and social environments that combined a passion for the past as well as for the future.

***

In 1996, Wei Shu had found the Master again at the Chinese University of Political Science and Law, in Beijing, where his philosophical thought was the focus of intense discussions. She had written in her intimate diary:

An exalting period rich in discussions and notably on the significance of the Confucian doctrine for our time. A millstone or a lever? We make contact again a bit clandestinely with the works of writers critical of the 1960s and 1970s. We have debates based on texts from the important revue Jintian, directed by the poets Bei Dao and Mang Ke, a revue that has known a strong influence, but a short life, at the end of the 1970s, then based on the writings of the supporters of the Fifth Modernization.

***

China was at the time living a major ideological revolution for herself and for the world. Deng's reform was henceforth assured. The desired opening was acquired. Its consequences, numerous and complex, established themselves forcefully. Among them was the burning need to demonstrate the political legitimacy of a State that had become the protagonist of economic liberalism poles apart from its ideological doctrine and its official rhetoric.

In truth, Marxism was in remission, in China as well as everywhere on the planet. It needed a new lease on life. This is what Deng had understood and resolved through a significant dose of values that had been until now the distinctive features of capitalism. By doing that, he breathed fresh air into the economy and allowed a socialism with Chinese colors to emerge, to set itself up and establish itself as a possible model for many countries.

Certain people, like the Prime Minister Zhao Ziyang, had believed in the political extensions of this new economic paradigm. Their aspirations would meet their Waterloo on Tian'anmen Square, in 1989. Deng Xiaoping, the architect of the economic opening up, became the adversary of the opening up policy, the organizer of the political *status quo*. The Beijing Spring was over!

China was them swept forward by a powerful economic elan without any apparent hesitation. It meant "carrying out a reform without questioning the socialist or capitalist nature of the reform."

The ideological space was open, yawning, waiting for a doctrine capable of filling a void with heavy risks for the Party, the State and the society. Kept in reserve, a national treasure was unearthed, the thinking of Confucius called upon to provide the conceptual framework and language, in short, the ritual of legitimacy. Here were the circumstances allowing that thinking to rise from its ashes.

So, two millenniums and a half after the Master's teaching, the new Asiatic power referred to it explicitly as a doctrine of universal scope, a reference liable to ensure cohesion and stability for Chinese society, and harmony for the international community.

Confucius lived in a troubled period, a period of great political upheavals. The Zhou dynasty had been dominating China at the time for seven centuries. Ensconced for more than three thousand years, it was then shaken by the rise of the Feudal States. Consequently, the Empire was in great danger of imploding and losing its power. As a witness to this unthinkable degradation, Confucius proposed rules and values likely to restore the lost harmony, a code of ethics capable of rebuilding social and political relationships, capable also of producing order, stability and prosperity.

***

Two and a half millenniums after the Master's teaching, as soon as she takes office in 2036, the President does not miss any opportunity to refer to it and thus to emphasize a filiation of which she considers herself a privileged trustee.

Harmony and responsibility are the key concepts in the thinking of Confucius. They are the same for Wei Shu. This binomial justifies the hierarchies and celebrates the connections. It proposes the development of personal virtues as values capable of carrying harmony far into the lives of people, from people to communities and from the latter to the whole of society.

By respecting these values and by fully exercising his very functions, the individual participates in an order that includes him while dominating him. Thus act the components of nature, each one being specific yet a fragment of an ensemble which, alone, endures in a kind of constitutive continuity.

For Confucius, the order in society, nature and the cosmos have repercussions on one another, they are the expression of an identical necessity, of an identical totality, of an identical unity. Such is harmony: the limit of what can be thought, the horizon of what can be accomplished by each one and by all, by each one and for all.

This thought offers an assured ethical framework for individuals, including leaders, various regroupings and society. It allows one to integrate modernity which, like a powerful tide, is invading China and cohabits with a national heritage and a rich patrimony. It provides the intelligentsia of the country with a doctrine flowing from national origins and arms the public discourse of the Chinese leaders with "exalting principles." According to the President's evaluation, harmony is at the center of a new constellation of references and proposals. Confucius has come back to life, his thought offering China and the world their metaphysical foundations.

***

At the university Wei Shu had frequented, these trends dominated teaching and research. Obviously, everyone measured the exact limit authorized for public debate. But it was indisputable that the philosophy of Confucius again occupied a central position.

Wei Shu had enrolled in a course devoted to the history of Confucianism in Chinese philosophical and political thought. Searching for a useful appropriateness between the thinking of Confucius and the necessities of the time, she dissected the interpretations of his immediate disciples Mencius and Xenzi, as well as those of Han Yu who reacted in the 7th century to the rise of the influence of Buddhism. Wei Shu was particularly interested in the interpretation of the thinker Zhu Xi who, in the 12th century, drew out a famous analysis of the Master's doctrine. This analysis was accepted as authoritative over the long haul and served as a reference for the imperial administration exams until the end of the Empire, in 1912.

Wei Shu also studied there the works of the philosophers Wang Yangming and Dai Zhen. The two advocated a return to the thinking of the Master, to the ethical and socioeconomic dimension of his teaching. She was excited by the endeavors to reform the Empire, in the 19th century, based on these teachings.

Each one of these interpretations was evaluated with great care, the deviations were ferreted out, the useful extensions explored. Slowly but inexorably, in circles where academicians, mandarins and politicians mingled, there emerged the immense and enduring influence of the thinking of Confucius in the long span of Chinese history.

Wei Shu was excited by this chronology, this perpetuity and this contemporaneity of the basic Confucian concepts. With some comrades, she had created a discussion group over which she presided. She had made some precious encounters there: Dai Zhen, Kant, Adam Smith, Locke, then her first love, a handsome foreign student of Arab origin, Bene, as everyone called him. He, too, was enthralled by Confucius.

She allowed herself to be captivated by this outstanding athlete who spoke a refined Mandarin and had a subtle knowledge of the history of the Middle Kingdom, also by the ease with which, as she said, he moved about in the territories of human thought. "Certain trends of thought assault us since the 19th century, Bene maintained, European positivism, Russian anarchism, dialectic materialism and so many others. These are dwarfs in comparison to Confucius."

Comparative calligraphies, languages, works of art from their two worlds were on the menu for these two young idealists searching for the levers to change the world. They would read together *The Book of the Face of the Earth* by al-Khwarismi published in Bagdad in the 9th century, the *Book of Examples* by Ibn Khaldoun and the poems by Du Fu, the great name in Chinese classical poetry, also the works of al-Sayyab, the great name in contemporary Arab poetry. During three happy years, as discreet lovers, they used to explore together, street by street, the beauties of Beijing and, at a distance, idealized those of Bagdad. In their way, they participated in the myth of the great cultural and religious metropolis that had been sustaining the collective imagination of the Muslim world for centuries.

***

Decades later, still discreet, the President will rarely refer to those years of "all the discoveries." Asked about her mastery of the Arabic language, she alludes vaguely to her years of university studies, then to comrades who came from far away Iraq. She recalls the vast circuits which, in the middle of the previous millennium, allowed not only silks, spices and earthenware to circulate, but also philosophical and scientific ideas, from China towards India and from India towards Africa, till Cairo, which was then the center of the vast Mameluke sultanate stretching from the Mediterranean to the Chinese frontier.

She will confide to a Palestinian woman journalist: "I remember with emotion that my Arab comrades and I shared the idea and the dream of the restoration of our reciprocal heritages and of their universal dimension. We were, all of us, obsessed by the same intentions: to re-establish the considerable contributions of our civilizations within the universal historical narrative and transform our immaterial respective patrimonies into systems adapted to our era. It seemed to us that these patrimonies had in common the idea that individual life and self-improvement are inseparable and an integral part of a mysterious and true encompassing structure. One of my comrades, Bene was his name, I believe, offered me a magnificent gift on the eve of his return to Bagdad. In his full and sweet voice, he recited for me a short poem by Ibn Al-Roumi, a famous writer of the 10th century:

In each era, a man
Unique offers an example to other men

In these times in which we live
He alone without a doubt is the model
'You know who this man is for me. I know who he is for you, our common Master, Confucius.'

***

Wei Shu was twenty-seven years old. China was amassing investments, commercial surpluses, scientific and technological advances. The young woman was living intensely these continuous transformations. In 2004, the country occupied fourth place among the world economies. Futurology studies, all converging, announced that it would occupy first place fifteen or twenty years later.

Holding a Masters degree in economics, connected to the Party, fluent in several languages, Wei Shu was aiming for a position as an analyst at the Ministry for Economic Planning and Development. She had successfully passed the required competition and was waiting for a notification that had still not come. Then finally it arrived: a large grey envelope of another era. A brief note informing her that she had been admitted to the long cycle of the Party's Central School, with the assurance of a position in the ministry of her choice at the end of the cycle. She consulted, hesitated and finally accepted.

***

Years later, she would write in her diary:

This choice was decisive. Devoted to the council of a state that comprises one fourth of humanity, the School enabled me to become familiar with and to master the keys of geopolitical and strategic analysis. It also enabled me to enlarge my network of friends and professional allies working in the ensemble of public domains and in all the regions of the country. Even today, I find myself meeting again comrades of that period in the provinces of Jilin, Sichuan, Hunan and many others still. This network remains very precious to me. Finally, the School gave me the opportunity to be associated with a laboratory of ideas and proposals without equal, the influence of which on national and international policy has been and is evident. I perfected there my knowledge of the Arabic language, I learned the English language and, during the first year, I visited the United States and Brazil; the second year, India and Morocco; then Israel, during my last year of studies in this institution for which I feel affection.

Finally, I found again my childhood friend Jie, the son of President Fang, whom I married afterwards, to the great contentment of our two families.

***

Located, since 2005, between the Summer Palace and the scientific and technological pole Zhongguancun, the Party Central School maintained the link between the two worlds which, at the time, made up China: the first based on a patina-inlaid tradition within the abundance of centuries and the second oriented towards the most obvious modernity; the first being a mandarinate rooted in thousands of years of history already unfolded and another, the new one, responsible for envisioning China's history to come.

Nestled in a series of ancient gardens, the School combined historic structures such as the Chouqxue Villa, the Tinqyu, Juquan and Fusham Pavillions, the bridges of the Five Steps, Wohong and Paulong, the Wonqji, Quinquan and Jianshi towers, as well as modern buildings including the monumental auditorium, the superb studies pavilion, a sumptuous gymnasium, a quality hotel and an immense greenhouse. Several bore the stamps of the greatest architects of their time, including Wang Shu, recipient of the Pritzker, the Nobel Prize for architecture.

The "light" foreground gave this unique ensemble a singular beauty, since at night there was a doubled outline of everything reflected in the water mirrors created to produce that effect.

This coexistence of the very old and the very modern could also be found in the School's collection of art works, which Shu admired and studied, *one work at a time, not as singular works standing alone, but as the unfinished construction and always in progress of the spirit of the Chinese nation that began about four thousand years ago,* she would write later on in her diary.

The painters Dai Jin, Hua Yan and Li Tang from the eras of the Qin and Ming dynasties were close to the most famous contemporaries, who made the art market shift from the west to the east of the planet, Ren Bonian, Qi Baishi, Zhang Daqian, Wang Xuetao, Zhang Xiaogang and many others.

"I carry this collection within me as though I had digitalized it in my mind and my heart, Wei Shu will say on a day of nostalgia. It was at the School that I acquired a passion for Chinese painting, the great unfolding of our landscapes and our faces, of our disappointments, successes and of the inexhaustible beauties of the galaxy that is China."

Under the direct authority of the Central Committee, geared to the continuous training of the present and future leaders of the Party and the government, the School was, at the turn of the millennium, the most influential *think tank* in the country and, perhaps, in the world. It supplied with ideas and projects not only the national government but those of the provinces, of the autonomous and administrative regions, and of the four municipalities enjoying a special status. It also sustained the Shanghai Association of Cooperation. Created in 2001 with five countries of Central Asia, this organization spread since then into the whole world and became a formidable lever for analyses and normative proposals just as the OECD had been for the West and Japan, in the previous century.

If the thought of Mao Zedong and Marxism dominated the teaching and research at the School from its creation, in 1952, this was no longer the case when Wei Shu was frequenting it.

It was the theses and policies of Deng Xiaoping that prevailed and carried far and wide their beneficial effects for China, whereas the Soviet Union was imploding and the globalization offensive of the West seemed to be triumphing. But one of the major effects of this global circulation of capital and goods was to accelerate the industrial, commercial and financial rise of China and to give her access to the most advanced communication technologies.

The degree course covered two large sectors: the world political and economic transformation taking place and the consequences, in the short and long term, of the United Nations series of international conferences held during the 1990s: the one in Rio on the environment and development; the one in Copenhagen on social development; the one in Cairo on world demography; the one in Beijing on the condition of women; the one in Vienna on human rights; the one in Istanbul on housing. If Washington was reticent about this continuous deployment of "supposedly world" problems, Beijing applauded the initiatives of the Secretary General of the United Nations, Boutros Boutros-Ghali. They represented as many circumstances as were necessary to establish the position of the new China, which accumulated international investments at an unrivalled pace, as well as industrial plants set up by the large western corporations in all the sectors that counted, technological transfers described as the most important in history.

The student belonged to the Chinese generation that had witnessed, in a short time frame, the biggest transformation in history affecting a quarter of humanity. In the words of Shu's father: "So now, the biggest poorest country in the world is in the process of becoming the foremost financial, commercial and economic power on the planet. Here, my darling, lies the responsibility of your generation: to reinforce this status and make it irreversible."

The Marxist ideology was still present in the Party's Central School. Indeed, it was subtly combined with the neo-Confucian thinking. The works of the intellectuals Tu Wei-ming, Fei Xiaotong, Tang Yijie and Chen Lai appeared on the short list of compulsory readings. If their proposals diverged, they still had common references, the thinking of the Master and his place in the identity of modern China, the works of the Master and his ability to stand in the way of the liberal-democratic ideology imposed on the world by the West.

As the spokeswoman in 2006 for a study group entrusted with the task of proposing an operational framework and elements of language to explain China's doctrine for the 21st century, Wei Shu had gained attention through the clarity and excellence of her work.

The potential upper crust intellectuals were invited to give testimony to the study group created by the Central School of the Party: specialists and respected sages such as the economists He Qinglian, Zhu Min and Zhhang Weiying, the writer Mai Tianshu and the historian Qian Chengdan. Also invited were specialized teams such as the forecasting cell of the Party, administrators of central institutions in the country, the provinces, the autonomous regions and municipalities.

Wei Shu reminded each group that it was important "to nurture the thinking of a country with the works and achievements that took place during its history spanning four millenniums, of a country that contained more than twice the population of Europe and four times that of the United States, about one quarter of the earth's humanity."

Foreign personalities such as Lee Kuan Yew, the father of Singapore, the Singapore diplomat Kishore Mahbubani, the female Indian writer Arundhati Roy and many others were also invited to share their analyses with the members of the committee. Reduced to the essential, the committee's mandate was completely contained in the replies to two questions that Wei Shu constantly asked: "What were the objectives for China in the second quarter of the 21st century and what would be the timetable for putting them into practice?

Then which doctrine was needed to further China's national ambition and its rise to power on the international level?"

In accordance with the thoughts of Deng Xiaoping and to continue applying them, the ideological imperatives were reasserted, then combined with the necessity to bear results. Lee Kuan Yew had hammered away all through his testimony at "three essential ideas" that the Committee would remember:

"Like never before in her history, China has at her disposal indispensable levers to produce growth and wealth. These levers are notably scientific and financial. The wealth produced must be distributed equitably, otherwise the country will become unmanageable. The challenge is considerable and urgent. There is no durable economic development without durable social development.

"Such is the major distinction between an effective society and its opposite. Let the benefits of growth serve the common good. And let everyone enjoy a return in keeping with his work, a return that sustains a verifiable and continuous improvement in everyone's standard of living. Already considerable, the present effort must be increased. Such is the condition for the development of a responsible citizenry, for the continuous progression of China's influence in the domains of science, technology and commerce which, all together, nourish growth and wealth.

"Finally, China must consider culture as the decisive element in its stability, its cohesion, its dynamism and its influence. Certainly, culture is not immutable. It has never been so. It will never be so. But what comes from the outside must be incorporated into the cultural ethos of the country. If you abandon the substance of your destiny as a distinctive human civilization, what guarantee will you have afterwards of being able to protect yourselves against the centrifugal forces present in all human communities?

"The family occupies the heart of your cultural heritage. It constitutes the base of it, the clan, the circle of partners and friends. According to Confucius, it constitutes the first critical relationship. All the laws, all the institutions cannot and will never be able to offer what it knows and teaches, remembers and frees, preserves and consecrates.

"To implement these policies, China must give priority to order, stability and responsibility. Consequently, there must be governance ensured by the best in the name of integrity, commitment, discipline and devotion. Such is the second critical relationship that Confucius puts forward. According to his teaching, authority must be strong and equitable, competent and stable."

The wise man from Singapore had sprinkled his speech with teachings taken from his own experience, from comparisons between the atomized approach of the West and the Asian approach based on solidarity. He had concluded with a long quotation from his old friend, the former German Chancellor Helmut Schmidt:

"It seems to me that the major elements of the cultural heritage of Confucius, and especially the importance attributed to meritocracy and the hierarchy taking into account age and experience, the insistence placed on education, on family and social cohesion do not need the European and North American religious ethic founded on very different spiritual concepts in order to reach the same levels of economic performance.

"Perhaps the West should admit that peoples living on other continents and rooted in other traditions can be fully happy even in the absence of democratic structures that Americans and Europeans deem indispensable.

Consequently, we must not ask China to profess democracy. We must however insist on the respect of the individual, the recognition of his dignity and his rights."

In the same breath, Lee Kuan Yew had pleaded for a strong leadership and had denounced the Welfare State, rejected "ideological refuges" and praised the singularity of human communities and their cultural heritage. The man had a freedom of tone that contrasted with the official kinds of rhetoric that were often predictable and repetitive.

Wei Shu was gripped by his fervent adherence, indeed his unshakeable certitude, concerning the responsibilities of people "without which everything that can be undertaken otherwise is condemned to failure and doomed to disaster;" she was impressed also by Lee Kuan Yew's insistence that people are not alone, but are constitutive fragments of ensembles which, in turn, define them.

Wei Shu had concluded the session by declaring that she "was strongly impressed by Lee Kuan Yew's presentation, by his ability to situate the evolution of Asia within the world system and identify the risks and possibilities of this evolution; also, by his ability to proclaim Asian values as essential contributions to our common security and shared development, as humanity's common possessions."

***

The phase of the working group's hearings devoted to exactly assessing China's rise to power in international affairs had excited Wei Shu. Except for certain differences of interpretation, all the futuristic scripts converged. It appeared to everyone that the United State's hegemony was in continuous decline, that this decline would reach a threshold of no-return during the 2020s and that there would be no stopping its acceleration until the year 2035. These were the converging conclusions reached by the Party's forecasting cell and by those monitored by the Asian Development Bank, the Japanese Economic Research Institute, the Nomura Research Institute and the University of the Future in India.

Wei Shu was struck by this convergence and had asked that an analysis of the decline of the United States, of their power and influence, be prepared for her. This analysis would constitute Annex 1 of the report *China in the 21ˢᵗ Century*, published at the end of 2006.

***

As the property of the Party's Central School, the report had quickly been taken over by the highest political circles in the country, which had culled the essential from the analyses and recommendations expressed in the previous study. These analyses and recommendations reinforced the ones made by the *Blue Book on Chinese Society* published in 2004 by the Institute for Social Research of the Chinese Academy of Social Sciences. The government of the Popular Republic was from that moment on superbly equipped for the next stages of the modernization of Chinese society.

***

At the end of 2007, the 16ᵗʰ Congress of the Party adopted a series of resolutions aimed at constructing "a society of a higher quality of life, a more developed economy, an improved democracy, a more advanced scientific and educational policy, and a more prosperous culture in a more harmonious society." Thank you, Wei Shu!

At that same congress, it was also proposed to reinforce the role of the Party leader in order to fully realize stability, growth and peace, the foundations of a harmonious society and world.

From the national level, the doctrine of harmony spread to the international one.

Already at the Asia-Africa Summit held in Jakarta in April 2005, as well as in the Joint Sino-Russian Declaration on the International Order in July 2005 and in a speech before the General Assembly of the United Nations, the same year, President Hu Jintao had successively evoked the harmony between the countries of the South and the harmony in the world. In December 2006, *The White Paper on National Defense in China* proclaimed world harmony as the great aspiration of the nation's military effort.

***

In a few short, decisive years, the doctrine of harmony "for China and the world" had established itself as a permanent reference and an objective that organized and stimulated the initiatives of the society, the Party and the government.

Among the proposals of Wei Shu's report, the one recommending the creation of a vast union of Asian nations had been received with interest, but scepticism. "For me, the President would say one day, this was the main thrust of the report, because the economic crisis of the 1990s had demonstrated beyond a shadow of a doubt that the analyses and interventions of the institutions, at Bretton Woods, had aggravated and prolonged the crisis at that time, because it appeared that it was necessary to distance ourselves, launch and pull off the transformation of Asia, that carried with it that of the world.

CHAPTER VII

JOHANNESBURG, 2027

IN 2024, AT FORTY-SEVEN, WEI SHU WAS PINCHING HERSELF, SINCE HER ascent in the Party and the government had been so rapid, rapid and spectacular.

The day after the publication of the report *China in the 21ˢᵗ Century*, she had joined the economic team of President Hu Jintao and, afterwards, had occupied successively the positions of Assistant Director of the Cabinet of the President of the Central Bank, of assistant Sherpa, then as Sherpa of China in international commercial negotiations and, finally, of Vice-Minister of the Economy.

In only a few years, her networks had expanded to the point of overflowing the frontiers of China. She extended invitations to the Taberna del Alabardero in Washington, "adored" the Café Marly in the heart of the Louvre, in Paris, and, in Geneva, settled into the Arcades, in the old city. In Berlin, she received at the Hasir in the Titanic Hotel and, in Beijing, a table was reserved for her at the Xi He Ya Ju restaurant, to the east of Changan Avenue. She was listening, learning, weaving her web on a planetary scale. She took as her own Lao Tzeu's ancient precept that she learned from her mother: *He who knows does not speak, he who speaks does not know.*

She had her rituals, her familiarities, her reservations, her words, too, of which there was one formula she repeated a thousand times and the effect of which was assured: "An encounter, she would repeat, is always the fruit of a celestial piece of luck."

She immobilized her guests in immutable categories: the fearful, the petty, the genuine, the relays. The latter were her preferred ones. They "never pronounce the word 'small' in front of a dwarf and know that it is useless to strike hard on a good drum."

"Words, words, words, I love them in all languages. They are the clothes of the spirit, redoubtable arms, an infinite force for whomever really masters them. They are like the fire held in reserve in volcanos that are supposedly extinct."

In the Party, in the government, at the international negotiating tables, people feared her silences, her naïve questions and, more than anything else, her precise, thorough, definitive arguments. "Dear friend, dear comrade, as they used to say, step back, and, you will see, everything opens up spontaneously."

About her intimate style of life, however, one knew little. A divorcee, a mother of two adolescents whose private life she protected "ferociously," in love with contemporary art, a polyglot, a feminist "for as long as it will take to make up for thousands of years of injustice," Wei Shu moved forward and left profound tracks. *An encounter is always the fruit of a celestial piece of luck...*

***

The celestial piece of luck had made her life capsize.

That "unique" year had been marked by the election of her father-in-law as President of the Party and the country. Having been Minister for Economic Planning and Development for two years, she agreed to move to New York and hold there, from January 2027, the position as Head of the Diplomatic Mission of the Popular Republic of China at the United Nations.

***

In Johannesburg, where she had fulfilled her first ministerial mission, the *shifu* who watched over her wherever she happened to be in the world had a short message passed on to her. She had read it and remained frozen, her eyes glued to the little piece of white paper in front of her. Then she had hidden her face for a long time in her large, well-cared-for hands, had risen slowly, had left the hall and, in a rare moment of intimacy in public, had allowed herself to be hugged by her faithful Persian companion.

"Jiang Sicong died in her sleep without suffering and without a struggle, he had whispered to her. I've spoken on the telephone to Ma. She kisses you ten times and is taking care of everything."

In the private salon which had been reserved for her at the OR Tambo airport in Johannesburg, Wei Shu, the powerful Minister of China's Economic Planning and Development, had become a little girl again, a child who had just lost her mother. As it was her custom in her moments of distress, she had launched into a long monologue to which the *shifu* listened without flinching. He knew that this torrent would save her.

"This woman was far more than my mother. I have lost the love of my life and China, her greatest historian. Of all the influences that have structured my life, Jian Sicong's occupies the very first rank. She enveloped me in a rare affection which I am suddenly missing and will miss until my last day. In her precise and vast way, she initiated me into the long history of our civilization, into the systems that have passed through the millenniums and into the insignificant ones that died out in the short term. You know her favorite statement: *Those who either don't have a past or no longer have one don't have a future.* It has become like a primal reference for me. From her immense knowledge, she extracted a body of teachings of great scope. They have structured my ability to judge people and events. They have nurtured my understanding of politics, of its mission and its functions. These teachings are still my markers for action. I am indebted to her and her mother, He Zuonen, for them more than I could ever say. Everything I know about the fury and the sweetness of the world comes to me from these women of fiery hearts, steel-like wills and sound, fertile judgments. For me, they embody what Chinese women have endured during our history. Also, what they have contributed to it which is impressive.

"Others will talk about what China and the world owe her, the magnitude of her contribution to the understanding of our history and that of the work of Sima Qian whose prestige has not dimmed in the past two thousand years. She accomplished her work during difficult times and endured untold sufferings. But the deepest sea has a bottom that can be measured by the highest summit of the mountain that it covers up. She knew successively the obscurity of the first and the brightness of the second. Jiang Sicong, China salutes your exemplary work; your daughter salutes your exemplary life."

***

Jiang Sicong was born in 1945 in the city of Wuhan, in the district of Nanghe, in the province of Hubei, at the centre of China. Her early childhood was apparently uneventful in a family torn between bourgeois atavism and the revolutionary movement led by Mao Zedong.

As a member of a business family in the neighboring province of Jiangxi, the mother of Jiang Sicong, He Zuonen, was appalled by the "divisional commander." As a child, she had heard "terrifying stories:" raids on homes belonging to her family; summary executions carried out in front of silent crowds; tortures and, especially, the burying of her grandfather under tons of rocks and grief.

Her father, a State civil servant, was for his part captivated by a speech announcing the destruction of the ancient China, corrupt and collaborationist, and by the emergence of an egalitarian China, finally the mistress of her wealth and her destiny.

Exalted, he had witnessed in Beijing, in October 1949, Mao proclaiming that China was communist from the balcony of the Gate of Celestial Peace. This gate opened onto Tian'anmen Square, right next to the Forbidden City where, for centuries, resided the emperors of China and their vast cohorts of relatives, courtesans, servants, flatterers and other mercenaries.

A terrible civil war was coming to an end. It had been marked by the Long March, that breathtaking and extraordinary human adventure; marked also by the cruel Japanese invasion.

Wei's grandfather was convinced that at last there would be peace, independence, and development! When he evoked the Long March, his voice would tremble. He had heard descriptions of vagabond hordes roaming around the continental country, coming up against rivers, mountains and hostile peasants, looking for a route that would lead to the freedom Mao had conjured up in *The New Democracy*.

This peasant's son carried around in his pouch all the political decadence, economic corruption and cultural backwardness that a century and a half had deposited as a sediment in the hearts and minds of the people of China. In it mingled the very true and the very false, the glorious narratives and all the others, the souls and the ripped open bodies, the profiles of the imaginary enemies and all the others, the traitors, the vice-ridden ones, those who were beyond redemption. All those who made one want to kill and to justify the killing.

Just a bit more to go, five hundred kilometres in the humid forest and five hundred more kilometres in the dried-up plain. Tibet was within their grasp. The next day, it would be Mongolia. Then imperialism would be dragged through the public squares and decapitated one hundred times rather than one. Let the day come when, according to Mao's words, "we will be able to tie up the monster."

The family was profoundly divided. Rare letters from 1949, coming from the capital, evoked the advent of a new era based on justice and equality. In Wuhan, it was difficult to share these enthusiastic outbursts, so widespread was the terror. Family members were hiding themselves in the low family home, expecting the worst. The Guangzhou-Beijing train unloaded refugees from the interior and stories of the worst abuses of power. Libraries and books were being set on fire, ancient buildings were being destroyed along with the works of art that were in them. Objects relating to China's cultural heritage were being buried in the nearby forests. Photos were being burned, as well as the ancestors' little altars... after being clandestinely photographed. Who safeguarded and who destroyed? Faces turned to granite and words got frozen in the inaudible rumbling.

The family was hanging on and, in 1955, it was reunited in Beijing. Jiang Sicong was ten years old. She moved upwards from the isolation in Wuhan to a life of privilege in the country's capital. The family fracture remained, however, silent, invisible but dominant. The father worked in the team of a high Party executive responsible for the rewriting of the school curriculums. As for the mother, she pursued her patient work as a historiographer devoted to the works and the influence of Sima Qian, the most illustrious of Chinese historians.

Both were living in their respective worlds, not knowing what the other was doing. They pursued their parallel lives, one plunged in the fantasies of a receding utopia destined to change the trajectory of humanity; the other, absorbed in understanding the historical development of "the world's first civilization."

The father's professional and political activities hardly had any effect on the family life. "He was absent, the mother would say one day to her daughter, "absent when he was not there, absent as well when he was there." Everyone knew that he kept up a second office, as one says in Africa, where resided an amorous lady militant or a mistress who was a militant, according to the fluctuating schedules of lives enveloped in sadness, lies and loud stifled cries.

The mother's activities touched off another kind of echo. As an active member of the historical circle guided by Wu Han, a great specialist of the history of the Ming dynasty that dominated China from 1368 to 1644, He Zuonen was the controversial author of essays devoted to the despotic emperors.

She constantly received colleagues and colleagues of colleagues. She debated everything, old regimes and the present one, traditions and new rituals, Confucius and Mao. "You know, she liked to repeat, "when a horse gallops alone, one cannot tell if he is swift or slow." This maxim had passed from generation to generation in the family.

Jiang Sicong grew up in this world, seemingly free to judge all these emperors, to weed out the ignoramuses, the petty ones, the genuine ones, the intermediaries. She grew up in a world where one dared say, even though it was in a whisper, that Mao had "the mouth of a Buddha and the heart of a serpent."

Through her father, she enjoyed advantages reserved for Party members, practiced Chinese classical dance, and got to learn calligraphy. She attended the school designated for the children of executives and respected to the letter her mother's instructions: *"He who knows does not speak, he who speaks does not know...* So, you will not speak. In any event, your round words cannot enter their square ears."

From her mother, she learned that an encounter is always "the fruit of a celestial stroke of luck," an opportunity to discipline one's judgement about the moral quality of other people, a theatre where no one is obliged to speak out if he is incapable of arousing commitment to his way of thinking. To succeed at that, thinking had to be precise, and, if incomplete, in the process of completion, but never definitive. It had to have a heart that beats, that becomes impassioned, then grows relaxed. It had to be alive!

Jian Sicong loved that woman and was loved in return by that free and rigorous, demanding and affectionate person who was incapable of "making anyone wear shoes that were too small." As concerned everyone and everything, except for her mother, she knew that good and evil existed together, and knew about their deceptive masks. She granted a second exception for her "lifelong" friend, Wu Yongehin, the daughter of Wu Han, who had become at the wrong time the assistant mayor of Beijing, for his greatest misfortune.

Two families, two homes, a sister! Jiang Sicong was a happy young woman. The two families attended the opera together, frequented the circuses and, supreme joy, did not miss a single theatrical performance. She enjoyed those protocols turned inside out, those pretentious and clumsy eunuchs, those exceedingly toadying actresses, painted with the thick makeup that whitened their faces, gave brightness to their red mouths and brilliance to their yellow or green eyes. A surplus of life and a surplus of death, the theatre was like tea. It left sediments in the minds and, when it hit the target, in the hearts. She liked the decors, the houses painted on canvasses that shook, the ephemeral arches, the immobile forests that witnessed the worst atrocities without the slightest emotion, the noise of a fox that was fleeing, a flight of birds that swooped down, a gust of wind that protested. She also liked those movements of bodies aroused by excesses of enchantment, the words that didn't manage to say what is not to be heard. Also, the sighs that ended like waves on seas of cotton bordered by somber and suddenly luminous cities.

***

Later on, her daughter Wei Shu would go with her friend from Bagdad to the little, almost clandestine theatre halls of the city. Three halls where readings of another time would take place, a time that would be bygone, and one that was going to come. Even later, Wei Shu and her *shifu* would frequent the Popular Theatre of Beijing and would applaud the first works of Gao Xingjian, whose *Bus Stop* was produced before the writer's departure, before his exile, before his Nobel Prize.

***

In the summer of 1961, Jing Sicong had attended, with the clan, the premiere of a play of a historical nature written by the father of her friend Wu Yongehin.

The aim was exemplary.

Between the peasants and the local authorities, a minister of the Ming regime takes the side of the former, acknowledging the validity of their grievances and condemning the abusive behaviour of the "local potentates." The audience had applauded this first act. Its attitude hardened when the emperor overturned his minister's decision and, proud and insensitive, turned against the peasants. The curtain fell on this malaise.

It would also fall on Jiang Sicgong's comfortable life. Five years later, this play served as a pretext for Mao to launch one of the most ferocious repressions in contemporary history. For the Great Helmsman and his flatterers, the Ming emperor was he himself.

The unthinkable sacrilege against his person was severely punished. The Cultural Revolution strove to break the narrow-minded revisionists, the partisans of feudalism, the ass lickers of imperial regimes, the Confucianist sermonizers, all those heretics who were dreaming of restoring their privileges and dared to oppose the thoughts and policies of Mao.

The first world of Jiang Sicong would be progressively destroyed. She had finished celebrating life. Day after day, the rumours were growing louder, the horror was taking shape and the monster was approaching.

At the University of Beijing, the first theatre of the revolution, she witnessed, frozen and incredulous, her friend Wu Hongehin's implacable and filthy indictment of her father, the exposure of the latter to the howling mob of Red Guards, to the humiliations he was made to endure. Dressed in a grotesque costume of the Ming Emperor, he had confessed his crimes and admitted, one hundred times rather than one, that he had wandered away tragically from the fertile and correct thinking of Mao Zedong.

Jiang Sicong had seen the father of her friend forced to take the famous throwing pose and, his body stretched to the limit, unstable and in pain, he was shaved like a common criminal. Unhinged children were shouting out to him: "Where the devil is your armband, where the devil is your armband?" She had slid into a paramilitary uniform, had put on the leather belt and fastened on her right arm the famous red armband. Haggard and rigid, she could hear the voice of Wu Han repeat one hundred times the text inscribed on an immense dazibao, a text which detailed and denounced his crimes.

Late at night, Jiang Sicong returned to the family home. Everything was devastated there: the library was emptied and hundreds of papers were sullied, torn apart, burnt. Hanging from the light fixture was an improvised dazibao denouncing the cuckolds of Confucius who were also the worshippers of Sima Qian. Twenty years of a unique research project were definitively ruined, the work of a lifetime, that of her mother, wiped out. The latter could not be found. Jiang Sicong was looking for a sign, a message. There were none. She would have to live in this void for a long time.

The radio was broadcasting again and again Mao's speech inviting the Red Guards to extend to the whole country the revolutionary movement the purpose of which was to shake up the world.

China was becoming an immense courthouse; the little red book, its unique code; the Red Guards, numbering one million in the summer of 1966 and twelve million two years later, became the insane litigants, the omniscient and omnipotent judges and executioners.

The hunt for infidels spread throughout the country. Professors, administrators, parents, children, village chiefs, monks, former and present spouses of "revisionists," minority representatives, Party managers, writers, librarians, artists and graduates of all the schools were persecuted, accused of betrayal, subjected to the most contemptible humiliations, disguised, tortured, raped, killed. Mao's old method had become fashionable again: group executions in front of exalted mobs.

Wearing the Red Guards uniform, Mao was spewing out slogans, including the famous "Bomb the headquarters." The great man was setting fire to volcanos, yet took the necessary precautions for his safety and ordered the Popular Liberation Army to restrain the hordes of unleashed children.

Hundreds of worker brigades were created with the order to knock down the pride of the tyrannical executives and managers and to regain control of the means of production. Everything had to be purified: family, school, business, administrations, speech, posters, language, culture, history, minds, hearts, life!

Everything, the body, the heart and the mind.

Everything had to be purified: books, music, films, libraries, theatres, operas, signs, designs, conversations, silences and all that was lodged between the two, the strange noises…

Everything had to be flushed out: the lukewarm, the silent, the runaways, the children of the bourgeoisie, those who felt nostalgia for the feudal system, the collectors of ancient objects, the readers of foreign books, the contemplators of obscene works.

Everything had to be denounced: American imperialism, paper tigers, revisionists, capitalism and other political maladies. In addition, the revolutionary inadequacy had to be compensated, the thinking of Mao glorified, and his person celebrated.

Confrontations pitted students against peasants, student brigades against worker brigades, children against parents, locally elected officials against citizen collectives. From certain of these confrontations arose uncontrolled local situations. Others were cunningly orchestrated by Mao himself.

Jiang Sicong lived like a recluse in the family home, where dozens of Red Guards had taken up residence. She was viewed as a neurotic, and, indeed, she had become one. She had feigned incoherence and had ended up by sinking into it; she had feigned delirium and had ended up recognizing herself as so afflicted.

Dressed in a paramilitary uniform, with the little red book in her hand, she would wander around in Beijing looking for her mother. She bumped into howling mobs parading under portraits of President Mao. She heard inflamed harangues denouncing the reactionaries, describing the advances the revolution was making in the Sichuan area, in the Fujian area, in Yunnan, and announcing the victory of the revolutionary policy of the glorious President.

On Tian'anmen Square, she listened to a sixteen-year-old adolescent announcing the shunting aside of the traitors, Peng Shen, the mayor of Beijing, Lu Dingyi, the propaganda agent, and Deng Xiaoping, the Secretary General of the Party.

"Those men have confessed their crimes. Tough, arrogant, fattened by privileges, we have not neglected anything to make them lower their masks."

"Those puppets have finally yielded."

"We have heard them describe a form of treason all the more alarming because they held positions of confidence within the Party. Today they are in prison. Tomorrow they will be judged and the day after they will be executed because of their treachery against the foremost revolutionary of the world, Mao Zedong."

Some of the accused chose suicide, frightened as they were by the outbursts that the mere mention of their names aroused. Others were liquidated while children and youth mobilized by the Great Helmsman and invoking their abundant crimes, screamed out their hatred. Hundreds of thousands of the "guilty" were sent off to the countryside. They were integrated there into "laborious masses" and re-educated in classes devoted to the thoughts of Mao that were generally led by young paramilitary.

***

After being sequestered in a technical school in Beijing, Jiang Sicong's mother had been deported at first to Xi'an, then to Kunming, in Yunnan, in the extreme southwest of the country.

The two voyages had been trying. In the midst of hundreds of Red Guards crowding the trains, the intellectuals to be re-educated were mocked, summoned up at night, during the day, alone or in a group, to answer the indictments of their guardians or perform the menial tasks the latter decided on. At each station, the guilty were exposed, railed at, constrained to describe their acts of treason, looking ridiculous in their awful getups, reduced by the crowd or by coercion to confess their acts of treachery.

When they reboarded the train, they were put together again in the same carriages and were obliged to recite revolutionary precepts in unison:

To produce well, one must think well.

To make the revolution, there must be a revolutionary party.

He who sides with the revolutionary people is a revolutionary.

After an interminable stop at the central station in Kunming, He Zuonen had been ordered to join, for the years to come, the ranks of the tobacco workers.

Some of her fellow-travelers had gone up with her till north of the superb Lake Dianchi, where the important silk roads going to Burma intersected. Others had taken other routes going in opposite directions towards the salt and phosphate mines, the real wealth of that large region.

In the tobacco plantations, He Zuonen could identify the origins of her imprisoned comrades: a large number of ethnic minority leaders, since the frontier of Yunnan bordered on Tibet, Vietnam, Laos, Burma, Nepal and India; but there were also directors of the famous Medical University of Kunming, renowned for its programs in medicine, its school for the teaching of the French language, its links to American universities and the Sorbonne, in Paris; finally, there were local Party chiefs, journalists and a very old woman who claimed to have served the Empress Cixi in the final years of her very long reign.

Jiang Sicong's mother sojourned for two long years in the tobacco plantations. Every day, without interruption or exception, the same schedule structured her life and that of her female and male companions. The day would begin as of five in the morning with a re-education session lasting two hours. Each one was invited to comment on an excerpt from Mao Zedong's reflections, to extract its significance for his own area of work, his institution, China and the world: also, to talk about the nature of his offense, the reasons and length of time he had deviated from the norm, which had led him to this school for re-education. At the end of the session, the guide separated the correct ones from the others, ranked the latter and meted out the punishments according to the gravity of the errors committed.

The day in the fields could then begin. It would last from eight to ten hours, however beautiful or bad the weather was, with the most difficult tasks assigned to the delinquents "with delicate hands." Finally, after a frugal meal, the day ended with a new re-education session.

Such had been He Zuonen's life, from the winter of 1967 to the winter of 1969, "one hundred million days or more," she would say afterwards of those years. Physical prostration, psychological collapse, moral distress, numbing of the mind: the heavy baggage of the heart and the weighty bales of tobacco had worn out this frail woman accustomed to speculating on the successive sets of circumstances affecting the dynasties and the way they took root in Chinese civilization.

Aside from the "doubtful associations" of which she was accused, what, then, was the fault she had committed that justified the punishment she received?

This question had obsessed her from the first to the last day of that severe internment from which she would never totally recover. What could be said about the more than four hundred re-education sessions, about the rigidity, the vanity and the obvious smugness of the officials; about the precariousness, the subordination and the anxiety of the incriminated? If the esprit de corps of the first was manifest, the solidarity of the others was inexistant.

When she returned to Beijing, He Zuonen recalled her exile.

"First of all, mistrust dominated all relationships without exception. For the re-education officials, we were the opponents of the thoughts and policies of Mao Zedong, counter-revolutionaries eager to re-establish the class society that existed before 1949.

"For the tobacco workers, we were criminals bringing adversity into their midst that they felt was more of a curse than a blessing. We were also in their eyes robbing them of their work and, from the first till the last day, viewed as foreigners coming from another world, having nothing to do with their own position.

For the incriminated, we were informers, spies, potential paramilitary and red guard agents responsible for their re-education. This phobia was skillfully maintained by the latter and their rigorous method of intimidation and terror: public assassinations, hangings of locals and foreigners, the disappearance of incriminated people, then the arrival of new conspirators; far off firing squads during the night. Everyone had to manage alone the almost certainty of his imminent death. In that context, the mistrust of every person and all was palpable in the gazes, the silences, the words held back, the rigidity of the bodies, the hearts and the minds.

"Some walled themselves up in absolute silence and, like robots, moved from the thinking of Mao to the mud in the tobacco fields with the same detachment and indifference. Others, exhausted by the work, desperate, abandoned themselves to the will of the "little masters," expecting an alleviation that would never come.

Finally, rage got hold of the most fragile, those people would stand up during the re-education sessions and howl out their hatred of the Great Helmsman and his accursed and "nauseating" regime. An old woman from Shanghai called out one day: "Kill me the way you have killed so many others, kill us all. When you will have killed us, they will kill you in turn. I worked in the secretariat of Jiang Qing, Mao's wife, and one day, in the train going from Beijing to Shanghai, I heard her say again and again: 'What's so important about a million deaths?' Me, I'm telling you, and tell it to all of yours, they will one day be submerged by the large number who refuse to see tarnished, destroyed and forgotten what a hundred generations of your ancestors have built up. Kill me as you have already killed so many others. Kill us all."

"Those people were led off to the dungeon, a long underground building from which one never came back in one piece. Tortured, they were brought back unrecognizable into our miserable encampments, paraded from one shack to another as an example, and coldly mowed down on the Square of the Glorious Revolution, in full view of all of us. Frightened by such violence, some strangled themselves with their clothing or strove to flee into the night, knowing that bullets would catch up with them in their desperate escape.

Once a month, the "little masters" informed the prisoners about the advances of the revolution, the luminous statements made by the President and about the favorable, enthusiastic, indeed dithyrambic assessments, formulated by the intellectuals of the whole world and, notably, the Europeans.

Fragment after fragment, Jiang Sicong would reconstruct her mother's sorrowful narrative. She noted her words and her expressions:

Fear like a shroud. The eclipse of any human compassion. The odour of the same bad breath that we had in common.

The successive collapse of wills, even of the ones that seemed most solid; impulsive confessions; the identification of accomplices; the detailed accounts of crimes never committed and, suddenly, the atrocious silence of the terror volunteers. The ban on any communication between us and with the outside world. Twenty-three months without any news of the family and friends, only obscene stories about our next-of-kin that the little masters would relate coldly, holding the papers in their hands.

During the first months, I would recite to myself excerpts from Teachings by Confucius *and some ancient poems. Then, my memory dried up. It emptied itself, leaving a hollow more opaque than bronze and in which nothing could weigh anchor, root itself, nourish itself. Every day, I saw, with my own eyes, all the misery that can befall us through the programmed imbalance of good and evil, the incommensurable drama of the negation of their indispensable coexistence.*

Sometimes, He Zuonen would remember the horrible poverty of the tobacco workers, the agony of women forced to twist twice around itself the head of their daughter as soon as she was born, the exhaustion of the men every evening of their life. In that China, "the sky remains low, very low, so low that it sometimes touches the ground, crushing all life."

Once she returned to Beijing, she thought about what she would be able to do to avoid transforming what she had experienced into a representation of the world, to extricate herself from a "dreadful" memory, according to her own term to designate what obsessed her day and night.

Would she relaunch her project devoted to the works of Sima Qian? She had wished to do so, then backed away from the cause of all her disappointments. Everything had become difficult for her: frequent contacts with her former colleagues, with the devastated archive documents, the memory effort, writing. The drama of starting up again proved impracticable. Long days were wasted in drawing up "unbearable" texts and in throwing them into the fire once night fell. "I'll get there," would repeat to herself with diminishing conviction the former tobacco fields worker, to the north of Lake Dianchi, in the agglomeration of Kunming.

Such was always the only road her stricken memory could take. She would return to it unceasingly. "Have I told you the story of the forest of Yunnan?"

101

"The day is particularly hard. There have been downpours for several days. Perfect weather to prune the plants. We work at it by moving with difficulty in the deep mud. That day I had joined forces with an old woman whose name I never found out. From the moment I arrived, she honored me with her constant spite. She was always screaming, her gaze was distant, her mouth toothless and slobbering: "Too fast, too slow, you rotten one!"

"That evening, on the way back, she had approached me and called out to me: "Rotten one! You, the Beijing scholar. I will swear that you don't know the story of the rocky forest. Me, I know it, and you, you don't know! Well, I will tell it to you.

"Hundreds of millions of years ago, a giant sea covered over all the lands of Yunnan. Me, I know, and you, you don't know. One day, a wind more violent than all the winds known until then froze the water in the great void of space. Everything that the water dissimulated froze, the fish, the other marine animals, the men, the sea plants, the shadow of the mountains and the shimmering of the forests. Thus was born the forest of stones, the greatest marvel in the world. Me, I know, and you, you don't know! Rotten one, you don't know and me, I know.' "

Time was passing. In the large house in Beijing, two steps from the Forbidden city, three generations of women lived together: He Zuonen, the grandmother whose memory had been devastated by so many fears, sorrows, visible and invisible burdens; her daughter, Jiang Sicong, the trustee of her mother's work, a work she was recreating, broadening and situating at the highest level of comprehension and interpretation of Chinese civilization; and her granddaughter, Wei Shu.

That youngest one was born with the modernization that Deng Xiaoping had wanted. Sixty years later, she would succeed him as the leader of what would be the foremost world power.

But she would also succeed those women, Jiang Sicong , her mother, "the love of her life," He Zuonen, her grandmother, Yu Shuhui, her great grandmother, "the connection of her life to the China before China."

One day, He Zuonen forgot to wake up. She had glided into the other world, alone in her dejection, alone in her night that had become interminable. The same day, Jiang Sicong swore she would accomplish the work launched a long time ago by her mother. She would devote her life to it. Fallen into disfavour in 1949, then again enjoying public favor, the works of Sima Qian became her sole occupation and preoccupation.

A great intellectual who had lived twenty-three centuries before, Sima Qian related the already long history of Chinese civilization that even then stretched out over two millenniums. He established the lineage of its leaders, its scientific advances and cultural assets. He also emphasized the geographical discoveries that had been made, especially under the Emperor Wudi, during maritime journeys undertaken towards the unknown lands where the immortals sojourn.

The works of Sima Qian were rare, precious, and major for China and humanity. They looked far into the human past and developed a global conception of human experience. From Antiquity to the 20ᵗʰ century, they had served as a model for successive generations of historians.

In the conclusion to her monumental study devoted to the perennial influence of Sima Qian and published in 1982, five years after the birth of her daughter, Jiang Sicong would write:

This work has placed history for all time at the center of Chinese civilization. He who wants to understand China must, first and foremost, acknowledge the base that history forms, not as a science among so many others, but as a center from which everything else exists and radiates outwards. Everything else, namely, philosophy, justice, culture, economics and any other domain of importance. And to understand this system of thought, it behooves us to know the works of Sima Qian, who is its undisputed designer. His historical memoirs have this fecundity.

Such was the destiny of Wei Shu's mother: to avenge her own mother by producing the work that she would have produced herself if the Cultural Revolution had not ruined her research and broken her spirit. To avenge her as well by setting against the will to annihilate the past—that central idea of the Cultural Revolution—the strong affirmation of the absolute richness of history. Because the latter is indeed more than the exact updating of the past. It is the foundation of an intention pursued constantly and never entirely realized in China and in the world: the intention to prevent violence that always remains in a latent state between men, factions, the powerful and those who aspire to replace them.

***

In the aircraft that had brought her back from Johannesburg to her mother's remains, Wei Shu had descended deeply into herself.

Her faithful companion had received a formal order: no matter what the reason or the rank of the seeker might be, no one was to have access to the ministerial suite.

Wei Shu was alone with herself, filled with an immense sorrow and abundant memories. The earlier ones were those of He Zuonen, her grandmother, a joyless old woman. Precise, vivid, happy , were those of Jiang Sicong, her loving, brilliant, radiant mother.

Two destinies so divergent, she thought, and, at the same time, two inseparable lives. If the project of one had become the life's work of the other, it is because the same passion had enriched their minds.

That passion had also become an inheritance, that of Sima Qian, He Zuonen and Jiang Sicong.

She had opened her diary and written:

Of all the influences that have structured my life, that of Jiang Sicong occupies the very first rank. I owe my mother more than I could ever express in words, she and her mother, He Zuonen. Everything I know about the fury and sweetness of the world comes to me from these two women with hearts like burning coals, with iron wills, and with sound and fertile judgments.

CHAPTER VIII

THE UNION OF ASIAN NATIONS

WITHIN THE PARTY AND THE GOVERNMENT, WEI SHU ACCELERATED HER crusade in favor of creating a Union of Asian Nations. "There are those who are against, the cowardly, the amnesiacs, the ignorant, who remember to varying degrees the campaign waged and lost by the Minister Wen Jiabo for a continental convergence." The Minister hammered her message at all levels possible. "Either we will reunite Asia, or certain countries will allow themselves to be seduced by a partnership that will escape our control. Barak Obama worked on that one."

This project was not new. The context had never been as favorable, however. With a confidence that was almost overblown, the minister became the advocate of the continent's unity.

"Powerful currents cross our minds and our countries and allow us to glimpse arrangements which, even yesterday, were inaccessible. When we really want it to be so, history is a bringer of change. Think of Europe in 1990, during the 1990s. The continent has been transformed by the convergent flows of intense energies. These have brought about the dislocation of the Soviet Union, the reunification of Germany, the establishment of the euro as a common currency and the Treaty of Maastricht as the first political architecture of the continent. Henceforth, the member countries of the European Union had at their disposal a policy of law-enforcement and judicial cooperation and a policy of common security. This is not to be sneezed at!

"Asia's turn has come. Our continent is in first place for everything that counts. If we desire it with passion, history will be the bringer of change for us as well, just as it was for the Old Continent. What a formula... the Old Continent!"

Within the Party's ranks, the issue had never been clearly inscribed in the important agendas. That was obviously proof it was an important matter. But things were changing. From the 2020s onward, the issue was the subject of all kinds of essential analyses and discussions and rose progressively to make the short list of national priorities.

The geopolitical transformations that Wei Shu and her clan's ambition foresaw were considerable and unfurled like an unexpected explosion. Indeed, the most populated region in the world was living in an accelerated mode a metamorphosis that even the day before seemed unthinkable. After a century or so of a heavy presence in the region, the United States had gradually abandoned it while maintaining a symbolic and episodic presence in the China Sea. Being in an accelerated decline, this physical presence was replaced by bellicose declarations which, according to the Minister's expression, "were falling into the void like shooting stars into ink-black nights."

After ninety years of a violent separation that had cost one million five hundred thousand deaths and produced twice as many collateral victims, the two Koreas had at last really moved closer to one another. Obviously, they were still far from a German-like reunification. The integration of the two economies was advancing at high speed, however. The project of a confederal union, also longstanding, was at the heart of discussions between Pyongyang and Seoul. At the request of China, Germany had acted as a mediator. Beijing's magisterium was henceforth assured, and the unification of the Koreas was inscribed there in the short list of Chinese priority objectives. The sunray policy was unfolding one area at a time and the sensitive issues were being negotiated three-ways: Pyongyang, Seoul and Beijing.

The Chinese diplomats who presided over the negotiation never closed a dossier until its resolution was found. The Minister had been precise on that matter.

"I am speaking to you in the name of the Party and the government. You have two years, maximum, to resolve a body of sensitive issues: the peace treaty, called the Koyo one, as a reminder of the name of a dynasty that was the architect of the first unification of the Korean nation, more than a thousand years ago; the management of the nuclear system which will make of the new Korea a member of the International Atomic Energy Agency; the costs of regrouping and realigning the many policies of the two former enemies. You can count on the good offices of Germany and on our unfailing support."

After very summarily seeking, with a glance, the views of all those present, the Minister rejoiced in the unanimity that was emerging and invited the two councils of ministers from North Korea as well as from South Korea who were present, to a great "Koyo" celebration at the Chinese embassy.

The festivities had been splendid. On screens unfolded superb images of the Taebaek summits, in the heart of the Mountain range that crosses and unites both Koreas. For centuries, these famous peaks had been venerated by all Koreans without distinction. Emerging from the slopes of these sacred mountains are two large rivers, the Han of the South and the Nakdong which also cross and unite the two fragments of the Korean country. The underlying message was transparent: the link between the two Koreas was indisputable, inspiring, alive, fruitful.

The dinner was coming to an end. The Minister had risen and, in her "musically metallic voice, that is to say, possessing a particular brilliance," as the *shifu* described it, had addressed these men and women of the country of the Calm Morning. All of them were ready to overturn, under pressure from her, the dogmas, policies and angry rhetoric, those toxic forms of oxygen that had ruined everything in the hearts and minds of many Koreans.

The Minister had put on a modernized version of the *hanbok*, the short jacket worn above the skirt, or *chima*. Re-imagined in this way, the traditional Korean dress "older than the sea," according to a popular legend, added to her great natural presence. She had asked that it be white, the color of Korea, and that suitable pendants be created, those long chains of silk adorned with semi-precious stones. She wore them with her necklace of black pearls.

The tables had been set up in the large salon of the embassy, and the interplay of mirrors multiplied the Minister's image. It seemed as though there were several of her conveying the same message:

"My dear friends, I will not make another speech, because I have already taken too much advantage of my speaking time these last two days.

"But I am anxious to convey to you the sentiment that has been dwelling within me ever since my country decided that the Asian Union would be an absolute priority. We are, you and us, the oldest civilizations still active in the world, radiating outwards, powerful not only on the material level but on all the others. This moment is ours. It is Asia's.

I thank you infinitely for your wise understanding and for sharing our conviction. It corresponds to the pressing needs of humanity, of our continent and of each one of the countries that is part of it. I have brought you a present which, I hope, will please you."

An immense screen had been unfurled and, for twenty minutes, an abundance of spectacular images had shown Asia as it had never been seen before.

Like an elegant choreography, the tableaus provided by satellites, drones and other machines capable of capturing the beauties of the planet had succeeded one another in a remarkable ballet. There were the extremities of this third of the world's lands above sea level that opened up onto all the continents on the planet; the Arctic Ocean and the Bering Straits to the north and the Indian ocean to the south, the Red Sea to the west and the Ural Mountains to the east, a half of which was anchored in Europe and the other, in Asia. Between these antipodes were the great plateaus, those of Anatolia and Tibet, and the vast plains of Manchuria. Then came the most important mountainous masses on the planet, the Himalayas, between the Taurus peaks and the archipelago of the large Sunda Islands.

Then one after the other the large cities of the continent glided past: Beirut, Osaka, Bagdad, Singapore, Busan, Hanoi, Bandung, Jakarta, Bangkok, Teheran, Istanbul and Xi'an, the most ancient city in China. Placed one next to the other, Seoul and Pyongyang had emerged, enveloped in a common opaqueness. Veiled at first, the images of the two rivals became progressively more distinctive and appeared in the same light. The Korean splendors blasted across the screen: the temple of Beomeosa, the fortress of Hwaseong, the Palace of the Sun in Kumsusan, the tombs of Koguryo and that of King Kongmin and, finally, the archipelago of Reconciliation. The image remained fixed, like a symbol of that splendid, vibrant, diverse and progressively united Asia.

The lights went up and the applause continued. The Minister had already left the premisses for Beijing.

***

In the aircraft that was bringing them back to the capital, the *shifu* had told Wei Shu that in her surprising garb, she had looked like a majestic icon "radiating what was true, just, indisputable." She slapped his hands and invited him to be silent "in order not to fill up the cabin with your silly statements, because then our aircraft would crash, inasmuch as your compliments, sir, are heavy and your arrangement of words, overwhelming." After a moment of silence, the *shifu* murmured that she was his preferred Minister from among all the ministers in the world, with or without the *hanbok* on the *chima*. "That's the sleeping pill I need," Wei Shu replied, while drawing closer to her *shifu*.

The latter asserted that the Korean operation was launched. The Minister acquiesced "slightly:" "It will be long, very long, because the waves of sorrows and lies that have flooded the hearts and minds are considerable. But, as the French say, we have crossed the threshold."

Running parallel to these major advances, Beijing was reconstructing its territorial unity by extirpating, one after the other, the effects of the pillages of history. China regained control of Hong Kong, lost to British hands as a result of the Sino-Japanese War of 1894-1895 and the defeat of the Qing Empire. She had already regained full control over Macao in 1987, putting an end to an occupation that had gone on for more than four centuries.

There remained Taiwan, the little island inhabited for four thousand years, the victim of a string of predators among whom were the Portuguese, the Dutch and the Japanese. In the very long term, the island was Chinese. In 1945, after the Japanese defeat, the United Nations had handed over the administration of it to Beijing and, in 1950, Mao had allowed the defeated nationalists to set themselves up there, temporarily… This "lease" came to an end after negotiations that formalized a relationship rich in all respects.

For more than a quarter of a century, Beijing and Taipei had become economic, financial, scientific and technological partners. If there was a time when Taiwan's technological development impressed the international community, it was clearly apparent, during the 2020s, that this development was inseparable from continental China's.

This was the result of international geopolitical evolutions, of Washington's withdrawal from Asia and the rise of the Popular Republic as a world power; this was also the result of colossal Taiwanese investments in continental China over the last half-century, of the symbiosis of researchers and laboratories on the two territories and of numerous common commercial delivery services; finally, it was the result of the continuous proliferation of unions between the inhabitants of the two societies, since the negotiations, impossible up till then, were concluded to the satisfaction of all parties. Taiwan, "an integral component of the Chinese nation," enjoyed the status of a "special autonomous region."

Some, in the Party, hesitated and pleaded in favour of creating a pan-Asiatic work commission. "It is out of the question, the Minister objected to her colleagues in the Political Bureau. Unless one gives credence to the ancient thesis that firecrackers drive away evil spirits. We are not at that stage, fortunately. The time has come to create an Asian union that will place us in the foremost rank of influence, prosperity and, that said between us, power."

"Indispensable," were the headlines in the largest online newspaper in the country. "Unrealizable," posted its clandestine rival. The Minister said nothing publicly except for witticisms about rivers that cross several countries: "Six for the Mekong; three for the Salouen and three also for the Brahmaputra, whereas the Yangzi Jiang and the Yellow River, these great continental water routes traverse abundant lands along six thousand three hundred kilometres for the first, and five thousand four hundred and sixty, for the second. Seen from the sky, they show us the path to follow."

The Minister called upon the services of her many media friends as well as all the others. Within a season or two, the national and regional cultural ecosystems had become enriched by a galaxy of events for which the continent was the common denominator. The machine produced what was expected of it.

As proof, the new Asia art market, that was set up with no expenses spared in Guangzhou, on the river of Pearls.

As proof, the great museums of China, which invited their Japanese, Korean, Vietnamese, Thai, Burmese and Filipino counterparts to exhibit in the Chinese establishments and in their own establishments the works that bore witness to reciprocal influences in ancient, modern and contemporary times.

As proof, the thousands of Confucius institutes that multiplied across the world colloquia, conferences and other manifestations illustrating "the Asiatic complementarities."

As proof, touring from one capital to the other, the progressive rise of the largest film festival in the world, sustained by an Asiatic star system that welcomed creators and artists from all the countries on the continent.

As proof, the Chinese universities, that were invited to rejoin the Confucius program based on the European Erasmus program and thus offering annually to two hundred thousand students the means to pursue their studies at university campuses in countries other than their own.

As proof, the Chinese cities that were invited to reinforce their twinning with cities on the continent where it already existed and to create it where it was lacking.

As proof, the world network CCTV, all its satellites and its relays on all the continents and in all the world's languages, broadcasting superb documentaries based on converging cultural, commercial and other interests within the Asian countries.

Against this singular backdrop, the Minister pursued her crusade in all the capitals of the countries on the continent. She whirled about, as she said herself, from Seoul to Hanoi, from Ulan-Bator to Phnom Penh, from Bangkok to Manila, from Pyongyang to Tokyo "in order to undo what had to be undone and connect what had to be connected."

The Japanese sequence was particularly sensitive. For Japan it meant putting an end diplomatically to its status as a privileged partner of the West and redefining itself progressively as a major partner of the Asiatic nations in this world alliance that China was seeking. "Otherwise, argued Wei Shu, who hoped to be heard, all their drillings will produce a muddied water that will never run clean."

Already, Japanese investments in China were exceeding, and by far, those that had been made in the Atlantic zone. Already, the great continental country was the top commercial client of the "little insular one." Finally, Japan, fearful for a long time in the face of Chinese military power, had the nuclear weapon at its disposal since 2031, an effective dissuasive instrument.

The Minister strongly insisted: "If you want your dreams to come true, don't sleep!" In private, she added: "To refuse would be the equivalent of preparing one's economic suicide."

With private and public dinners, private missions and public missions, successful visits and aborted visits, private conferences and public conferences, huge colloquia and minuscule colloquia, friendly notes and stiff notes, the project was moving forward, moving backwards, then moving forward again. Wei Shu was profoundly convinced that it was in China's interest to formalize her links with the whole body of countries on the continent. She was also convinced that it would provide a formidable lever for the next stages in her country's affirmation, as well as for pursuing her personal political itinerary.

The creation of a vast political and economic community, the Union of Asian Nations, was progressively taking shape. It was based on ties that had become close, almost intimate, between China and her immediate and continental neighbors and those, innumerable, that brought together business heads, scientists, intellectuals, artists and athletes of the Asiatic countries.

The project was progressively absorbing one by one the nine members of the Association of Southeast Asia Nations (ASEAN), and Japan was coming there by stages. A reunified Korea found in it guaranties for its security and the reconstruction of its identity.

***

Signed in Beijing on February 6, 2032, the Union of Asian Nations is the work of Wei Shu. The new economic space constitutes the most important free trade zone in history. It counts for 60% of the world's GDP, controls more than 55% of the whole planet's research budgets, houses a majority of so-called world business enterprises and enjoys a market of three billion debt-free consumers. Here then is the biggest economic coalition in history.

When addressing the delegates, the Minister Wei Shu had resumed as follows the geopolitical state of each country present, of their new union and of the world:

"For a long time each one of our countries was forced to rethink itself, indeed redefine itself in relation to the West, to its imperative decrees, its fire power and the constant use of force which fortunately it no longer is the only one to possess. Each member country of our Union has been a victim, these past centuries, of these destructive outbursts against us, outbursts that were nuclear, military, financial and commercial, outbursts that were also immaterial, historic, linguistic and cultural.

These times are past. Now we have the nations of Asia finally reunited as a result of vast ventures converging, vast ventures that some judged unrealistic and carrying heavy risks.

"Our common values can be found in our respective DNAs and in our Common DNA. Just like processes that enrich substances and ideas, our values have been developed, refined and consolidated during the very long duration of history.

"Our nations are ancient. They are the most ancient of humanity. Their narratives spread out over millenniums. Every one of them has benefited from a specific alchemy that has transformed its own trajectory, material and immaterial, demographic, political, social and intellectual into a distinctive identity. Nevertheless, our nations have also benefited from a common alchemy, that immense spiritual, philosophical, social, scientific and technological coming and going between our countries, from yesterday to today.

"These criss-crossing transmissions explain, beyond all our frontiers and all our conflicts, the existence, so manifest and powerful, of the Asiatic identity which, in its way, defines us as well. It does more than define us. It has a mission to bring to the world a shared security, order, development and growth, these blessings that arise from harmony.

"And what if Asia made of this century the century of peace? The century during which we left behind definitively "fear and shortages" on a planetary scale. What a contrast with the explosions of the last century which, from Europe, have sullied the body, mind and heart of the world! The time has come for the West to rethink itself in depth, to redefine itself like an organism, for what is left of it and for each of the countries that compose it, in relation to the Asiatic community that we form henceforth."

The speech made the headlines in everything that was published in the world, virtually or in print.

"85% positive, the *shifu* had proclaimed, plus the hesitant and the old ones, the very old descendants of the *Wall Street Journal.*"

--I thought these archeologists had vanished, the Minister let slip. Their importance comes from the way others see them. Otherwise, they don't exist. We must, therefore, ignore them exuberantly."

The Minister greeted all her counterparts one by one and rushed into her long Hongqi limousine. Quickly, to the family home, near the Forbidden City.

***

That night, the *shifu's* birthday was being celebrated. An impressive cluster of intimates, the big club of political friends, a few ambassadors who counted and the Chinese ambassador in Washington. Also present were the friends from the opera, the theatre, the world of art and "other necessities." Two buffets were set up. One was laden with sumptuous Iranian dishes: barley soup; rice with beans, the famous *baghali polo;* a version of eggplant caviar, *kashke bademjan; coucou sib za-mini,* a kind of potato and herbs omelette; *borani bademjan,* yogurt with eggplant that was the Minister's favourite, with *koofteh,* meatballs stuffed with eggs, while the *shifu* was searching covetously for *koresh fesenjan,* a chicken stew with nuts that his grandmother would make for him, for his birthday, when he was a child in Ispahan.

On the other side, the Chinese buffet also offered its abundant marvels: soups with fine rice noodles, with shredded stag meat, with almonds, with soja milk and with beef marrow, the *Shuang jiao yu tou* for the fish lovers; mapo tuofu; *niango, jian bing,* a big plate of marinated vegetables and *you tiao* borrowed from street food and of which the *shifu* was particularly fond. There was also chicken kung pao, shrimp with rice noodles and garlic, and a *hot pot* so rich that from a distance it resembled a large polychrome palette that added to the ambiance of abundance.

The Minister was clearly happy with this feast that celebrated the birthday of her "very, very dear friend," on the very day when the Asian Union was consecrated. She ate little, as was her custom. "She eats through her ears," the *shifu* had said, using an old expression designating those who talk about food more than they consume it.

The dinner was coming to an end. In the library, Wei Shu was correcting a paper that she would present the next day before the members of parliament. She incorporated into it some references to the preamble of the Singapore Declaration, signed in November 2028.

Considering the disagreements that have divided us as arising from the expansion designs of the western powers during the second half of the second millennium and exacerbated during the 20ᵗʰ century;

Considering these disagreements resolved in their entirety following the Inchon Accords and the solemn Kyoto Declaration;

Considering our common responsibilities in the monitoring of the affairs of Asia and the world;

We, the people of Asia, proclaim the conditions propitious for negotiating a treaty designed to create the Union of Asian Nations and invite our partners in the region to join with us in the phases to come.

The Union of Asian Nations will constitute the foremost political and economic community in the world. It will be based on the recognition of equality among the contracting nations and all nations, the affirmation of equal and inalienable rights.

This recognition and this affirmation constitute the foundation of our union, the basis for the protection of rights and their indispensable complement, individual, national and henceforth continental responsibility. They will be our common reference in international negotiations. They constitute for our nations and for all nations, the guarantee of security, justice and shared development.

It took less than a half-century for President Deng's vision to give again to China the certitude that her ancient conviction was still valid and that she occupied the center of the world.

***

In Europe and America, this profound change was noted with open uneasiness.

In a declaration judged "unfortunate," the American President had evoked the new conditions for regional cooperation in Asia and the old ties uniting America and the Pacific countries in order to wish that the Union to come would be inspired by the recognized international norms and would give a prominent place to the constitutional state and to rights and freedoms. The spokesman of the Chinese government was content to simply smile and borrow an answer from Wei Shu: "We are waiting for you. You must succeed in your re-education. A major one, it might take a long time."

The German Chancellor, a signatory of the general agreement of economic and cultural cooperation with Beijing, had wished the Asian nations complete success, "in the very area where the European ones have failed." He duly noted the new references for the whole body of international negotiations decided by the new Union of the Asian Nations.

In Moscow, they were content to plagiarize Berlin, but had trouble concealing fears arising from the emergence of such a power at the oriental edges of the former frontiers of the Empire that Russia used to control.

Wei Shu had been the mistress of this successful planetary negotiation. For her *shifu* who, all this time, supposedly "played the role of the Empire's principal eunuch," she read with detachment the cables that expressed the reactions of the various people.

She proposed sending the American President a "very little bonsai" as a present with this note: "Thank you for reminding us that clouds produce rain and that rain produces clouds."

CHAPITRE IX

CAMBRIDGE, MASSACHUSETTS, 2037

INAUGURATING AN EXCEPTIONAL CYCLE OF LECTURES TO MARK THE FOUR hundredth anniversary of its founding, Harvard University welcomes Wei Shu, the new President of the Popular Republic of China, in its famous Sanders Theatre. This 4th of October 2037 will enter the history books.

The event will be retransmitted in real time on the campuses of four hundred universities on five continents. Thus, the President will be present simultaneously, in the hologram mode, on the grounds of the most important universities in the world. The event will also be broadcast on the Web, on the whole body of American channels and on the diverse venues of the Chinese international channel CCTV as well as on its one hundred and fifty-eight affiliated or partner networks.

The columnists, bloggers and other influential people speculate, comment, predict, analyze, assess and judge a speech that is still to come. As for their part, all the paparazzi in the world are waiting in ambush to snap the definitive photo of the President and her *shifu*, the photo of the woman who is presented indifferently as the most powerful in the world or as the most beautiful.

Rarely has a "private visit" by a head of State given rise to such demanding negotiations. In a first stage, the Chinese President had refused the invitation, since the conditions for the trip were judged insufficient or unsatisfactory. The file is closed, they said in Beijing, almost closed, they hoped in Cambridge.

In a second stage, the Chinese ambassador in Washington had brought up before the President of Harvard "a list of non-negotiable demands" that could lead the Chinese government to reassess its decision. The list was substantial.

That the government of the United States offer assurances that no important public speech will take place seventy-two hours before and seventy-two hours after the President's lecture at Harvard University, unless there was an exceptional situation recognized by the two parties.

That the invitation be reformulated in the Chinese language, since, moreover, it is understood that Wei Shu's presentation would also be made "in the world's first language" and that it would be broadcast live over the whole body of American television networks using the services of the Chinese President's interpreters.

That the Vice-President of the United States, the President of the House of Representatives and the accredited members of the diplomatic corps in Washington be invited and warmly encouraged to attend the President's presentation. As one New York commentator was saying at the time: "Those who are absent will remains so for life."

That the national anthem of the Popular Republic of China be performed by the Boston Symphony Orchestra at the beginning of the ceremony.

That on the day following the lecture, the President of the United States make the trip from Washington to Boston for a strictly private encounter with the head of the Chinese State. Finally, that this encounter should not give rise to any press release from the two parties, either together or separately, before the President's press conference scheduled on her return to the Chinese capital.

***

Three months of intense negotiations produced positive results, the famous university having set into motion the whole body of its national and international networks, including the Chinese one, the effectiveness of which is notorious. It is said that several rising stars in the Chinese Communist Party have done graduate studies at the Ash Center of the Kennedy School of Government at Harvard University after having obtained a first diploma at the University of Political Science and Law, situated in Beijing.

The press release appearing simultaneously in Beijing, Washington and Cambridge confirmed the visit:

Her Excellency Madame Wei Shu, President of the Popular Republic of China, will make a private visit to Harvard University, in the city of Cambridge in the State of Massachusetts, in the United States, on the occasion of the four hundredth anniversary of the founding of the University.

The President will sojourn for forty-eight hours on American soil. She will give on October 4, 2037, at 16 hours, the inaugural speech of this commemoration that will continue all year. The next day, at 10h30, the President will meet privately with the President of the United States, who will make the trip to Boston.

***

In the large semi-circular auditorium of the Sanders Theatre, the *Veritas* pennant of the University separates or unites the red flag with the five stars and the striped flag with the fifty stars. On the stage was a gigantic bouquet of white flowers offered by the Association of Chinese students in the United States.

Borrowing from the Barak and Michelle Obama model of lecture-spectacles during the 2010-2020 years, the first part of the encounter is made up of projections showing the President in different parts of the world before, during and after her investiture. Elegant, multi-lingual, the center of attraction, applauded, effective in the stinging replies she gives to journalists' questions, funny, insistent then detached, she is always skillful and always a politician: "Forget your octave. Henceforth, you will have to think of your music in terms of the Chinese five-tone scale or renounce music."

The message is clear. The scale, the tone and the music are Chinese from now on!

The lady ambassador from Nigeria leans towards her neighbor, the lady ambassador from Korea, and whispers in her ear: "A fashion show or a geopolitical show?

-Inseparable and redoubtable," answers the envoy from Seoul.

Radiant, Wei Shu enters through the rear door, walks up the central alley, greets the guests, "1000% of the American intelligentsia, 1000% of the country's billionaires and 1000% of the accredited diplomat-spies in Washington," according to the remark made by Che Se at breakfast, at the Liberty Hotel, transformed into a fortress for the event. Accompanied by the President of the University and a few personalities of the delegation, surrounded by her twelve bodyguards, the President advances slowly towards the front of the large auditorium to continuous great applause from a public interested in and intrigued by this out-of-the-ordinary personage who enjoys an exceptional popularity rating in her country and in the world.

But who really is this woman at the head of the foremost power in the world? Why did she accept this uncommon invitation, for the purpose of what strategies and what messages? "Machiavelli or Confucius?" is the headline in thick print of the *Boston Globe*, one of the most influential dailies in the United States.

The President is wearing a modern version of the Chinese *qipao*, a close-fitting dress with long, large sleeves that allow for wide variations in gesture. Intriguing, theatrical, "presidential and almost imperial," according to Che Se. "No, no, very imperial," the *shifu* whispers to him. The President's emerald *qipao* appears on all of the world's screens. The fashion is launched. Orders pile up at Alibaba and Amazon, and in the world's swanky boutiques.

The President beams forth. She moves forward slowly and, writes the *Washington Post*, draws off to herself almost all the oxygen." Che Se comes close to her and hands her a note. "The lecture will be seen in the next forty-eight hours by more than two hundred million people!" She looks at him absent-mindedly and shoots back at him ironically: "Only!"

The Chinese delegation takes its place in the very first rows, to her left. She is welcomed by categories: ministers and high-ranking civil servants, chancellors of universities and specialized institutes, heads of national cultural institutions, presidents of large technological and scientific groups, including all those that have research projects with the researchers of Harvard and the Massachusetts Institute of Technology. Finally, historians and political pundits who, in the days to come, will participate in an international symposium devoted to the comparative analysis of the Chinese and American narratives concerning the history of the Chinese revolution in 1949.

The subject is close to the President's heart. "I owe it to my mother and my grandmother, she insists, both drew close to 'great knowledge,' which allows for the visionary grasping of life past and life to come. Such is the profit derived from the loving study of history."

At the very beginning of her address, she invites the participants in the symposium to hold a second session in the city of Xi'an, formerly named Chang'an, or the City of Eternal Peace. There can be found the burial place of the first emperor of China, Qin Shi Huangdi, and the famous terra cotta army which, in the bowels of the earth, has been protecting him for twenty-two centuries.

The lady conductor of the prestigious Boston Symphony Orchestra makes her entrance, the musicians rise. The applause is generous, then silence prevails. At that moment the President rises and everyone does with her. The first measures of *The March of the Volunteers* reverberate, the national anthem of the Popular Republic of China. The work is predictable, both violent and soft, like so many other works of its kind.

Arise, we no longer want to be slaves.
With our flesh we are going to build our new wall...
Arise! Arise! Arise!
We, who are as one, brave the enemies' fire.
Forward! Forward! Forward!

In multiple translations, the text of the national anthem appears on hundreds of millions of screens in the world. *Forward! Forward! Forward!*

Che Se writes on his portable telephone:

Less bloody than the French one, which evokes "the impure blood that waters our fields" or the American one, asserting that "their blood has washed the stains of their hideous marks."

There follows a projection which, in a short time span, illustrates the perpetuity of the Chinese state from the first emperor who held power twenty-four centuries ago till the empress who, within a few instants, will speak, a speech awaited everywhere in the world.

The lights go up again. Already on stage, Wei Shu receives a long ovation that she allows to go on while there appear on two giant screens on either side of her the first images of her speech. Eloquent, adding a continuous emotion to the text, the images follow one another at a slow pace, then a swifter one, just like the text that they illustrate. The *shifu* will say: "The perfume within the flower!"

The speech is not short. In a first phase, the Present celebrates science.

"This immemorial undertaking illustrates the capacities of humanity to satisfy its fundamental needs. "Science has ceaselessly sought to identify, to shed light on and master the opaque portions of the human adventure. Also, to understand, to harness and orient the natural energies that irrigate the many systems which are indispensable for life, for all lives, those of millions of communities that carry our collective and personal destinies, those of eight billion humans who share our planet.

"Thanks to science, our ties to nature, in a first phase, and to the cosmos, in a second, have continuously been enriched. True, these advances have taken place in some particular part of the word, but they are accustomed to merrily cross all frontiers. Then their contents become humanity's common heritage.

"Over a lengthy time-span, science that developed in China has travelled through Asiatic circuits, then African ones, from India to Egypt, and ended up in Andalusia and, from there, it crossed Europe and took the first boat to America. At each of these stages, it profited from enrichments in order to finally become a universal science. I find very moving this long traversing of worlds to reach the minds of billions of human beings. Such are mathematics, chemistry, modern physics and those clusters of by-products which participate in maintaining life: from meteorology to medicine, from aeronautics to spatial engineering, from digital technology to artificial intelligence.

"Other streams, flowing from other matrices, the European, the American, the indigenous which, in that last case, reminds us of the absolute complementarity of all that the Universe contains, have also followed the paths of Science's long trek across the world. We have already experienced the benefits in my country that has become again one of the most important providers and one of the first beneficiaries of scientific advances.

"It is these vast movements ultimately converging that I have come to celebrate with you. As well as the important part that your university and all the universities in the world have played. I salute your irreplaceable contribution, and theirs, to this universal quest pursued here for four centuries, and pursued in the world since its origins.

"A mystery of the antipodes, your university has for a long time occupied the first place among the universities of the world, according to the so-called Shanghai classification. I salute it and celebrate it in the name of all those who have benefited from its contribution as well as in the name of those who have been interested in this immemorial quest for truth.

"When your university was born, in 1636, my country had at the time one hundred million inhabitants and yours, a little more than fifty thousand. You were then involved in populating and occupying the territory of the American continent. We were then establishing the last phase of the imperial regime that has governed the Chinese nation for three millenniums. What advances since then, yes, what advances, in America and China!

"With those who, across the world, celebrate with us, I share my personal list of projects that we must imperatively bring to fruition in this century, by basing our work on the formidable scientific levers we have at our disposal.

"We must imperatively make up for the tragic lost time by restoring the environmental balances of our planet, which are those of life; by creating a body of norms that aim to preserve its hydric resources-this common gift of humanity being in grave danger; by building the boldest cooperation in history so that all may benefit from the goods that space contains while there is still time; by completing urgently the common juridical instruments so that responsibility and security may be guaranteed for everyone in the digital era where nearly 70% of human activity is happening, by establishing a constraining equalization policy between the nations of the world to ensure an equitable sharing of the wealth produced. Finally, we must endow the community of nations with new institutions capable of setting in motion and achieving these vital objectives for the preservation of life, of all lives, of our lives."

The social medias collapse. The comments on the President's words and other subjects associated with her presence at Harvard are legion. The most breathtaking issues discussed take place side by side with simplistic issues, for example concerning the emerald color of her *qipao*. Some wonder about her list of projects for the 21st century, whereas others criticize her makeup. One internaut writes: "The Chinese no longer want to be slaves, according to their national anthem," "no, neither do we…so why this army of terra cotta soldiers?" Several have recourse to all of the software at their disposal to alter for better or worse, in color, in black, in white, in copper, in caricatural form the face of Wei Shu. In certain malevolent reconstitutions, she is seen so close to her *shifu* that they become nothing more than one body. Here references to history are criticized, as well as her tendentious way of situating the origin of science in China. "A homage to Harvard or a homage to China?"

Some love unconditionally, approve, applaud, congratulate, celebrate, quote passages and enrich them with their own exaltations. Other detest in their entirety "this spaced-out tone so far from lived realities; then "these settings up of comparisons of the world's regions with China as though the latter were a universal gauge."

The big wheel of opinions, judgments, words, explanations, readings and re-readings goes round at great speed. On this day, it captures nothing else, or little more, than the words of that women addressing the world from Sanders Theatre in Harvard University, in the city of Cambridge in the State of Massachusetts, in America. That woman is the President of the Popular Republic of China, just recently ranked as the first among international powers.

From science, she moves on to life. The internauts have lots of material to fill their screens and they will do it.

"Friends, all this scientific knowledge and their many different forms are aiming at one same target, life, to understand, protect, preserve and ensure that it commands absolute respect. *"What is life?"* asked a British scientist, in a famous text that my father made me read more than thirty years ago. In truth, humanity has been asking this question from the very beginning. It is on the curriculums of all the great schools as well as those of life and of societies. It surges upwards from all societies, including mine, and from the teachings of the oldest institution of higher learning in the world, the University of Nanking. For over twenty centuries, with perseverance and integrity, the researchers of that university have been taking part in this universal quest.

I have come all the way to you to celebrate, with you, the sciences of life in all their forms. They provide the yeast for humanity's future advances. At present, we must take into account the complementarity of all living beings, be they vegetal, animal or human. We must also agree on common norms to orient our choices in those sciences which are advancing at great speed, from biological engineering to bio-software, from molecular biology to neurobiological science and to so-called genetics of the fourth generation.

"My country will propose, in the near future, the in-depth overhaul of existent agreements in this domain and which we judge outdated owing to the major scientific advances of the last decades. Our common legal and statutory mechanisms have fallen tragically behind. This is for us, the governments of the world, and for you, the universities of the world, a vital, high-priority and common project.

"I have come all the way to you to tell you the importance that we attribute to the immemorial links connecting researchers of our countries with the international community of researchers; links that were established and enriched during the extended time of history and that have contributed to the understanding, protection and preservation of life. Know that China will support the enrichment of these links, since humanity has such a need for this sharing to preserve and protect life."

Internauts have contradictory material here, everything that relates to life being so sensitive. "What is this plea, if not the forerunner for regulating behaviour in order to live freely?" "Finally, a policy that goes right to the essential!" Between these two opposing assessments, there is a whole gamut of questionings, sentiments, fears, because life appears "mysterious" to all, "fragile," for the majority, "unbearable" for some, "a bottomless well of anguish," according to a sexagenarian from Texas, "a rich adventure," as an old Polish lady says.

The last part of the President's address arouses torrents of commentaries, because the idea of a new universality undermines secular heritages and because this idea appears fruitful in other parts of the world.

"Your invitation offers me the opportunity to formulate again the message of my country to yours and to the world.

"One half-century ago, under the authority of President Deng Xiaoping, China judged that the time had come to put its vast material and immaterial, scientific and cultural resources in the service of a new position of co-development for humanity. Obviously, this decision corresponded to certain national and international circumstances. But it had been in a latent state for several centuries.

"In accordance with the convergence of opposites in which we believe, this universal law, the reconstruction of the world is now being initiated after a long period of deconstruction. For at least three centuries, from inside and outside of China, successive evolutions have been announcing it, then have been petering out with an equal fervor. The reconstruction had to happen and it happened. In a short space of time, shorter than a human generation, the ensemble composed of all the available resources for a shared co-development has seen a radical transformation without equivalent in history. It is said of algorithms that they are powerful, and indeed they are. But I am talking to you about the irreplaceable power of human determination. In less than a generation, the latter has presided over a transformation of many essential sectors in my country. You know it, you are living it, its effects are being felt and will continue being felt during the long extension of time and for the whole human family.

"I plead before you for an extension of the philosophy of President Deng, whose inestimable contribution to the progression of humanity makes him one of the great figures in contemporary history.

"From China, the impetus surging from his intelligence and will has crossed frontiers and regenerated economic balances in favor of the greatest number.

"I met President Deng during my early childhood. My father, as you know, was one of his closest collaborators. I am inspired by his thinking which, by combining principles and pragmatism, has regenerated fundamental social and economic principles in favor of billions of people in my country and in the world. His influence is unparalleled in contemporary history, in the history of China and of humanity. Unfinished, certainly, but irreversible, the transformations I have evoked previously correspond to the objectives and results that this giant had established and foreseen.

"A stable and democratic China where citizens have rights because they also have duties.

"A stable and prosperous China concerned with fairness in sharing the wealth produced.

"As you know, poverty will be extirpated from China before the end of the century. Here you have a considerable accomplishment.

"This great country, so-called poor and economically backwards, has hoisted itself in barely a half-century up to the first ranks for wealth and economic, financial, commercial and technological ability. The effort expended, immense, is the end result of a concerted policy between the Central State and the governments of the twenty-three Chinese provinces. Their contractual contributions have made it possible to double in two decades our commitments in the domains of educations and health care.

"Our policy of equalization payments between the regions and the redistribution among individuals has been completed by massive investments in social development, without which economic development is a delusion. Last year, the number of our university graduates was one and a half times superior to the population of your neighbor, Canada.

"We are indebted to a great party, the Chinese Communist Party, boasting one hundred and fifty million members, for this policy of stability, prosperity, sharing and socialist democracy. We are indebted to a great people, the Chinese people, for having accepted it over the long haul. I have total confidence in these two pillars which are our Party and our people.

"Our policies are constantly revitalized through a vast system of consultations, discussions and proposals with which my fellow-citizens are associated, if such is their wish. Nothing escapes this permanent discussion between the citizens, the innumerable Party cells, the organizations of our civil society and the public powers on all levels. Our political system is one of the most decentralized in the world: 70% of public resources emerge from provincial budgets and local governments.

"One does not govern China without an indispensable policy of continuous dialogue with all the provincial and local powers. One does not define national norms or a wealth-sharing formula without the inseparable participation of all the parties involved.

"This necessity has embedded itself in the way we think of our country and our governance over the past three millenniums. It has surged forward with strength every time there has been an attempt to erase it. One cannot understand 1949 and 1978 if one is not familiar with our attachment to this doctrine.

The most ancient Chinese philosophy and the most modern version view order or, better still, harmonious organization as the supreme principle. This principle structures our social systems, from the family to the collectivity to which we first belong up to the national community. It presides over the political organization at all levels, from the most modest of communes to our megacities, from the local Party cells to its highest authority. It has produced miracles like the harmonious almost tripling of our population, from five hundred million people in 1950 to one billion four hundred million people today.

"For more than thirty years now, teams of the great university that has brought us together today have been measuring and analyzing the satisfaction ratings of my countrymen towards their government. You perhaps are aware that this rate has been very high since President Deng reprogrammed the imaginary dimension and the vital energies of the country.

"What remains for us to complete is considerable. According to the enlightened opinion of a large number, including several who are here with us today, the quality of our governance, the balance between public power and the initiative of the private sector, our consensual political choices and the richness of our moral values have produced convincing, diversified and durable results that have changed China and the world.

"Some point to this entity as a model. I leave this assessment with them. What is uppermost for us, however, is that the philosophy of President Dent has become international and that everywhere are being reprogramed the imaginary dimensions and the vital energies of each nation, of all humanity.

"The synthesis between the values of the different civilizations which, together, form the common endowment of humanity is waiting to be effected. For four centuries, the largest number of people have been asked to conform: But, according to the eloquent expression of the great Senegalese writer, Senghor, 'memory is irreducible' and it cannot be eternally contained.

"The time for conformity is passed. What must replace it imperatively is a demanding search for harmony and its multiple manifestations which law has the authority to clarify, bring together and protect.

"We have put forward clearly and determinedly the imperious necessity to reappraise, indeed, to overhaul the multilateral international organizations and institutions. They, too, in their entirety, reflect another era. I make of this overhaul a priority of my presidency, in continuity with the proposals formulated five years ago by my predecessor, in his speech in Rabat.

"With our partners of Greater Asia, we have created the most important economic community in the history of humanity. It accounts for a third of the human family and more than 55% of world trade. Its members share a same promise: the setting aside forever of memories of past conflicts, of all past conflicts, and the definitive commitment to a new era, an era of harmony. Our will is made of granite. Our international institutions, including the highly respected Shanghai Association of Cooperation, welcome the majority of the world's nations. As a result of this cause- effect relationship, our integrated system calls for the converging and harmonization of the so-called international system, which is falling apart, as its sad performances show daily.

"Such as it has become, the UN system has lost the confidence of the nations and the people of the world. Its reform is a delusion, a long march towards the abyss. It has consisted in lifting a stone in order to let it fall to the ground, one time, a hundred times, a thousand times. Who today can grant the slightest credibility to this endless parody? China has withdrawn from it, convinced that one cannot produced sculpture out of rotten wood.

From my observation post, I can see the long road we have had to travel in order to take cognizance of the totality of human experiences. This cognizance would signal a new start for humanity. My country has frequented for a long, indeed very long time that eternal entity known as history. It can be compared to 'the north star that remains immobile, while the other stars revolve around it,' according to the expression of Confucius. No country, no matter how powerful, neither yours nor mine, can claim to stop alone a new reorganization of the world.

"We know that history never stops, that our common task is to insert in it for good the idea and reality of harmony. We know that science is our true lever that will enable the blossoming forth of lives, of all lives.

"I respectfully salute the contribution of your four times centenary university to this eternal venture."

The audience applauded at length. Che Se observes the elite of the American elite giving an ovation to this woman who came from China to tell them some truths that are difficult to hear. *Beyond politeness, what then is this great applause concealing?* he wonders.

During the evening, he asked the question in the principal salon of the Liberty where the President is receiving her national guests at dinner. If there is obviously unanimity concerning the quality of the contents of her speech, opinions are mixed about the acceptance of the vision of history that has already unfolded and remains to unfold that it conveys. A consensus forms around the following ideas. Many have appreciated "the praise of science, the brief statement concerning the priorities of the century, the celebration of life and the plea for the creation of new international institutions. But some have undoubtedly strong reservations about the narrative evoking the advances of China, the richness of its political system and its millennial fixation on harmony in all things and on universal harmony.

Later, in their suite, the *shifu* will play the part of the queen's jester as only he can.

"Madame President, this applause also marks a genuine admiration for your remarkable national and international career, your major accomplishments and your direct and refined style, your natural assurance, an assurance of which I have been a privileged witness for a quarter of a century; the same assurance at the Vatican, among the Zulus, the Russians, at the British royal bunker as at the pizzeria on 9th Avenue, in New York, where you told me for the first time that I was someone exceptional, completely exceptional."

CHAPTER X

QIN SHI: FROM NEW YORK TO SHANGHAI

"*STEP BACK, AND EVERYTHING OPENS UP SPONTANEOUSLY.*" THE President repeats the ancient proverb as though it were a mantra. She theorizes for her principal collaborators: "With the benefit of hindsight there emerges a time for strategic analysis, assessing trustworthy allies and opposing forces, then identifying the ways and means to enrich the first group and make the second melt away. Friends, this process is less costly than beginning again, renouncing or accepting defeat. Those who know me are aware that the ideas of starting again, of renouncing or accepting defeat run absolutely counter to my nature." The method will achieve exacting standards without precedent during the reign of Wie Shu.

The day she takes office, she receives at dinner her civil cabinet in the renovated salons of the presidential dwelling. Perfume burners with designs of vertically intertwining dragons waft a delicate country-like odor, an old family recipe of dried flowers and bamboo roots, which, from her natal village, has made it around the world.

Relaxed and friendly, she welcomes all those who have been or will be her closest collaborators. She inquires about their children's progress and their elders' health. She comments on the works of art from the national collections that she has selected herself, "sensitive to the ones that oscillate between incertitude and certitude, which is truly the function of art. For a long time I have been extremely partial to Ren Xiong's self-portrait, which is normally exhibited in the Palace Museum in the Forbidden City; also to the *Rock and Hemerocal* by Zang

Heng, and finally, to the *Eternal Dialogue* by Zhang Jian-Jun, a work that caused a scandal at the Shanghai Biennial in 2002. The valuations have changed a great deal since then. Tell me, which Chinese artist has done the six dynamic ink sketches contained in this large frame?

-Don't answer, it's a trap! Calls out the *shifu*.

-They are taken from the *People* series by Suh Se-ok otherwise known as Sanjeong, one of the greatest contemporary Korean painters. I discovered it in New York, and these works have been with me since my mission at the United Nations. For me, they embody human energy, fragile and irreplaceable."

***

The guests have sat down at the tables. Wei Shu is radiant in a mauve tunic and her long necklace of black pearls inherited from her mother. Behind her, an astonishing fresco reproducing the famous categories of the *Bencao gangmu* pharmacopeia shows large, red-crested cranes striking all possible poses. This impeccable reproduction of a masterpiece of the 16th century confers an unexpected lightness to the place. One imagines oneself in a large aviary where its occupants remain immobile, waiting to depart. The President will have minute reproductions made as gifts to her visitors. She will do the same for the large vase of longevity adorned with ten thousand characters, the original of which has been at the Palace Museum since 1692. For some very rare guests, she has had reproduced and translated excerpts from *Four Stores*, a superb compilation of Chinese intellectual patrimonies commissioned by the Emperor Qianlong in the 18th century. According to oral tradition, the great work benefited from contributions from two thousand literary scholars. One finds in it Confucian classics, historical, philosophical and scientific treatises as well as great literary works. The box is a genuine work of art. On pale grey leather is reproduced the Yu Ji Tu, the very old map of the voyages made by Yu Gong that show the Chinese coast and the many jade-colored water routes that criss-cross over an infinite territory. The President's collaborators have an idea of the link she has created or entertains with her visitors according to whether she offers them "beautiful but anonymous" presents selected by the Ministry of Foreign Affairs or these "admirable" reproductions of superb works of art that she has chosen herself.

The work session will begin. Here, punctuality carries the weight of oxygen. If late, it is better to abstain; twice late and you are summoned to a farewell party!

The major domos have placed three teapots on the tables, to heat, infuse and serve the tea respectively, which has been the imperial drink for thirteen centuries. Poets have glorified it as an elixir ensuring self-control and guaranteeing serenity. The President relates that her maternal grandmother would recite the texts of the "great poet Baisao" of the 18th century who, all his life, celebrated the chucking out of powder tea and the return of Chinese tea, and also the return of the ceremony which, necessarily, accompanies its tasting.

According to the protocol adopted and the choice of pearl colored or twisted leaves, one can detect the degree of hospitality intended. In order not to make mistakes, one must read the antique opuscule devoted to the tea protocol in the Imperial City. They say that everything is changing in China, except the tea protocol. Everyone must take notice of this.

The President prefers sun-dried green tea from the region of Suzhou, in the province of Jiangsu, and wok-grilled white tea from Hangzhou, in the province of Zhejiang, which she consumes in large quantities. Wherever she is, there are reserves of these teas at her disposal, and also of vapor-dried black tea from Pu'er from the province of Yunnan which, she says, helps her overcome jetlag. A somewhat thick tea with milk is made with it, according to recipes perfected during the time of the Empress Cixi.

Che Se rises and, speaking to the President, assures her of "the total availability of all those who, starting today, belong to her private cabinet, and belong to China's first team. Consequently, they are jointly responsible for the success of the mandate that begins today. They will have to think rightly and apply the ancient teachings which have ensured the continuity of Chinese civilization: dignified private behaviour; respect for people in authority and kindness towards the largest number of people."

She thanks him, she says, as "one thanks a faithful companion." Then she addresses them all.

"Know that I have chosen you with great care. I expect from you unfailing loyalty, frankness at all times and exemplary service for the partners and clients for whom you are responsible. Also, be continuously attentive to the Chinese people, to their needs, their moods and aspirations as well as to the Party that sustains them and the government that sets the common rules. We are at the controls of the most extraordinary political experience in history. Therefore, do not content yourself with simply knowing, but assess, integrate and love this knowledge and transform it for the benefit of the largest number of people."

After a silence, she adds:

"Che Se has evoked the ancient teachings of our country. There is one that is particularly dear to me. My mother taught me the thoughts of Xun Zi, on whom one of the greatest thinkers of our country fixed his gaze. I rely on each one of you to make it real in our era. For the respected thinker, everything is based on knowledge, which fortifies judgment and willpower. This self-perfection carries over onto the proper functioning of intimate communities, including the family, and the latter leaves an imprint on local governances and finally on the functioning of the State.

"The status of China, its reputation and responsibility exclude the right to make mistakes. They exclude it for the person who is speaking to you and for each one of you. I will be judged and you will be as well by this standard. Friends, I raise my glass to our future successes. Long live the people of China and our beloved country!"

Around the tables, every member of the elite is represented: the Party has lent its director of communications and four of its best analysts; the Ministry of Science and Technology, a high-level team in charge especially of the expansion policy of Chinanet and the fifth generation of artificial intelligence; the Ministry of Finance, specialists in the domain of investments and international trade; the Ministry of Foreign Affairs, a team of diplomats empowered to follow and enrich China's relationships with the two hundred and two sovereign countries, Asiatic regional institutions and a selection of international organizations.

The director of the civil cabinet is explicit:

"You are all bound by the strictest confidentiality. I say again, by the strictest confidentiality. Only my office has the authority to release correspondences, documents, texts, diverse contributions of the presidency for the deliberations of the Party, the government, national and international institutions, foreign representations and medias. A hundred percent of what is agreed upon at the presidency level is classified as State secret, first category. This is the kind of thing one must not forget, if one does not wish to be forgotten for all eternity.

"At the slightest misdemeanor, you will be subjected to the *koutou*, that old imperial practice that consists in three genuflexions, three successive prostrations, separated by three audible blows to the head on the ground. Know that you will not be able to choose the ground!

"Long live the Popular Republic!" called out the President, provoking uncontrollable laughter among the guests.

"Every presidential project is submitted to the Priorities Committee of the Council of Affairs of State to be evaluated. Once this evaluation is completed, a follow-up bureau of three members is immediately formed. This bureau chooses the agent or agents to launch the project, determine its financing structure and an imperative timetable for its realization. Whoever wants to remain on the useful lists must be aware of it. To ignore it means choosing to disappear forever from these lists!

Venturing through the mazes and the requirements of State Security, one of the very first projects that Wei Shu submits to the Priorities Committee is "a highly confidential and absolutely high priority project," aimed at transferring the United Nations Organization from New York to Shanghai. The members of the Civil Cabinet have heard the President's message.

"This transfer constitutes one of the major objectives of my presidency. I consider it essential because of the present and durable state of international relations, the place of our country in the affairs of the world, and its place and responsibility regarding notably common security and shared development. We must imperatively pick up this challenge. We owe it to the more than one hundred generations who have shaped the nation's DNA. We owe it to them for having acknowledged and consolidated their values in a unique ensemble of which I am a trustee with the Party and the government. We owe it also to the recent generations. They have brought China to the forefront of immaterial and material wealth, and consequently to the forefront of responsibility. Finally, today, 55% of the world's populations lives in Asia—80% in Africa and Asia—against 13% for Europe and America. It is time to draw out the symbolic and political consequences of this essential fact."

Like all things in China, the operation, which will bear the name of Qin Shi Huangdi, is a river with several banks that move away and draw closer according to the fluctuation of circumstances. Between the sober first evocation in an official document and the spectacular offensive of the new President, who designates this operation as the major objective of her presidency in matters of international politics, the banks have drawn closer.

Before the Party's Central Committee, Wei Shu declares: "The time has come to realize on a world-wide scale what Qin Shi Huangdi accomplished for China two thousand years ago, namely, the unification of the kingdom around common rules and norms."

This project is not new. For two decades, it has been the object of abundant speculations in the chancelleries, the social networks and the medias. It has given rise to innumerable colloquiums and other encounters in university milieus. Government spokesmen have often evoked it as an element of a "futurological pedagogy," according to the statement of a Vice-Minister of Foreign Affairs.

For two years now, the corridors of the glass palace, in New York, have been buzzing with rumors about the intensive international campaign led by China with the aim to make the transfer happen.

The Chinese officials posted at the United Nations repeat this rumor to anyone who wants to listen to it. They never deny it when they are questioned. It even happens that they ask the question and give the answer.

Officially, the Chinese government has not yet adopted a point of view even if it encourages, finances and allows its representatives to participate in colloquiums, symposiums and public debates of all kinds that would move the "Lego bricks" from New York to Shanghai.

The election of Wei Shu changes the game. The new President has strong convictions and unique knowledge concerning "that absolute necessity"—convictions and knowledge acquired notably during her mandate as head of the diplomatic mission of China at the United Nations.

This case made to the Priorities Committee for the transfer of the United Nations Organization from New York to Shanghai, right at the beginning of her mandate, proves it clearly. If the powerful Chinese governmental machine gets hold of the project, and it does get hold of it, it then becomes one of the high-priority objectives of the foremost world power.

In the report that Wei Shu herself revised and updated, the President describes three components of the initiative officially called "Operation Qin Shi Huangdi." In working groups, networks of all kinds, medias, papers of all kinds presented by speakers, among humorists and cartoonists, the diminutive "Qin Shi" asserts itself and becomes the popular universal name of this initiative. The slogan, "Operation Qin Shi, from New York to Shanghai," is spelled out in letters of light, from Times Square to Red Square, from the Champs-Élysées to Copacabana, from the Promenade des Anglais to Mumbai up to Revolution Square in Havana.

The three components are inseparable. In the first place, the state of political obsolescence of the glass palace in Manhattan is manifest. Proof of it is the fact that the Security Council has been incapable of deciding on the candidate for the position of Secretary General of the United Nations these past two years. At this level, the temporary replacement is a sign of disinterest.

And the weakness of the temporary replacement is strategic, except for the person holding that position. World powers reproach her for not making up her mind: "After all, you are the Secretary General of the United Nations." And when she decides, they remind her: "After all, you are not the Secretary General, you are only the Acting Secretary."

Secondly, the relationships between the Council and the Secretariat General have become distant and superficial. A real fissure separates the two complementary entities, as though the two hemispheres of the political brain of humanity had been drawn apart.

From New York to Geneva, from Vienna to Rome, from Nairobi to Paris, wherever one looks closely at the institutions of the United Nations family, all situated in the West, with one or two possible exceptions, the same state of prostration stands out. *Some of them*, one reads in the report, *are in a state of clinical death; others pretend to exist, being without resources, without a following and without a future.*

Mechanisms voided of all substance, they are pitiful, with their rituals of another era, their language devoid of resonance and their disconnect from populations, nations and governments. Moreover, the latter, in their overwhelming majority, only react on a formal level—when they react at all—to the demands, appeals and injunctions of these organizations that are supposed to inform, direct and ensure the security and development of the human family.

The President comments: "In the villages of my childhood, they said: *Chicken feathers and onion peelings... It's just junk!*"

Finally, this obsolescent state of the multilateral organizations born after the Second World War weighs heavily and dangerously on common security and shared development.

Never, since the beginning of the millennium, has the burning necessity of reconstructing the international system been shared by so many countries, just like the necessity of placing at its center an institution reflecting the present and predictable state of the world, of its needs and its aspirations. This institution will have to take into consideration the place that Africa and Greater Asia occupy henceforth and, in its midst, China. Together, these two fragments of humanity account for 80% of the world's population.

World-wide opinion polls, multinational petitions, resolutions from multiple professional organizations, labor cooperatives and others, motions made by national assemblies and parliaments, are all part of a long list of those who, over the past fifty years, have wished for these reforms that never came, in lieu of the establishment of new institutions.

Although they still considered this enterprise as eminent, the powers of the time, during the second half of the 20th century, simply went through the motions of supporting it. They quickly exhausted their legitimacy, their will and ability. Those responsible for the failure of the United Nations no longer dispose of any credit to resuscitate it.

The Chinese President is determined:

"In June 2015, our country had presented an exhaustive plan to reform the United Nations. It was mocked and shoved aside. Our counterparts, permanent members of the Security Council, have exhausted themselves presenting reform plans that were quickly abandoned one after the other, because they reflected the realities of a bygone era. The picked up heavy stones that they let fall on their own feet."

Only China possesses the political, diplomatic and financial means required to undertake this work of reconstruction and succeed at it. "The time has come, the President believes, to use for this objective the dividends from the massive material and immaterial investments China has made in the world, during this past half-century. The time has come for China to "put wind into the wind," according to the ancestral formula taken up by President Deng.

"We are going to produce a synthesis never seen before in the history of humanity. Between submitting or mastering, our choice is clear, between disorder or harmony, our responsibility is obvious."

She points out to her close collaborators the presence on her desk of a singular sculpture, the *Miniature Mountain*, from the Ming era. "Here we are engaged, friends, in climbing an invisible mountain that this miniature will remind us of constantly. I will need a solidly roped team. Going backwards is not possible. It would mean that China is humiliating China."

The strategists of the presidency and the Party decide upon an option called "absolute presence." There is a long list of events and places chosen to announce the good news. "Our list is like the presence we wish for, absolute, declares Che Se. All the western networks and all of ours that dominate world discussions, all international conferences devoted to science, technology, ecology, international relations, contemporary history and international law are represented. Our contemporaries must witness a torrent on the network of networks."

Financed at a high level and led by an initiatives committee depending directly on the presidency, the operation fuses two ventures of great scope: the deployment of a public diplomacy program based on the knowledge and the recognition of China as a civilization, and the organization, in Beijing, of the first conference of the member nations of the Asian Union of Nations.

***

In a secret report from 2032, but "sunk" ten times rather than one, the European Union describes as follows the diplomatic mechanism that China possesses to conduct its campaign:

In the service of its open diplomacy program, China has at its disposal a redoubtable armada: the vastest network of diplomatic representations in the world, including three hundred embassies, nine hundred consulates and four hundred so-called offices of economic cooperation.

The Chinese government also disposes of a thousand Confucius institutes, whose purpose is to promote Chinese civilization, culture and language, and set up in an ensemble of cities chosen for their cultural prestige. Each one of these institutes sustains a participation structure including universities, graduate schools, laboratories, research centres and other agencies, totalling for the network of Confucius institutes more than one hundred and twenty thousand partners.

Finally, the Chinese government can also count on the contribution of numerous radio and television conglomerates broadcasting in more than one hundred languages in all parts of the world, and on its presence on the Internet that has no equal.

This whole body of tools is completed by a unified influence combining the resources of the Ministry of Foreign Affairs and of International Trade and ensuring China's presence in economic fairs, congresses and international cultural events.

Finally, thousands of Chinese businesses and banks as well as foreign ones with interests in China are expected to make contributions. These sponsorships run through a vast gamut: galas, awards for excellence, group voyages, participation in various regional or national manifestations, preferential financings. For the year 2032, in Europe alone, these contributions exceed one hundred million euros.

Brought into convergency, these powerful means sustain a program that aims to present the history of China as molded by external influences and bearing beneficial influences for the world. All-powerful, the idea of synthesis and harmony dominates this immense choreography of interests.

***

Here is the China from immemorial times, the China of mythical sovereigns from the third millennium to the era when the ancient kingdoms were pacified—pacified and unified—the China of essential achievements: from writing to the mastery of iron and bronze; from the fabrication of ceramics to the weaving of silk; from work on precious jade to the use of coal as a fuel.

Here are the acquisitions of the China of the historical era: unified legal systems, converging calendars, common norms concerning weights and measures. Here, also, are the invention and deployment of a public administration applying its rules to dozens of millions of people over vast territories.

Here is the map of China designated then as "the little country." It expands through the centuries until the present frontiers, towards the Northeast, Manchuria, and further towards the country of the Tunguska; towards the northwest, Mongolia, central Asia, Russia and, further still, Eurasia; towards the southwest, Pakistan, Bhutan, Bangladesh and, beyond the high plateaus of Tibet, the immensity of India; still further south towards Burma, Laos and Vietnam. Finally, to the east of the China Sea, Japan, Korea and Taiwan, and to the extreme south, the far-off archipelagos making up the Philippines today, Malaysia and Indonesia. At the center of these worlds, eternal China.

Everything moves through these multiple frontiers that separate and unify those distinct worlds, men, customs, ideas, languages, technologies, ways of governing, legal systems, philosophies and religions. Everything moves from China towards those societies near and far, and from the latter back to China.

In the long term, China absorbed Islam as early as the 7th century, Buddhism from the 3rd century and Christianity from the 13th century.

Here is China of the Middle Ages, the most extended empire in the world. Her mastery of the network of roads in Central Asia and her access to the seas of the planet make of this empire an economic entity without equal where circulate material and immaterial goods produced in all parts of the world.

Here is China submerged by invasions; the Mongols who, in 1279, take control of the country and deploy there the essential elements of their culture; the Manchus are next, in 1443, who dominate her until the beginning of the 20th century; then come the western powers and Japan which, from the 16th century, occupy her and impose on her the famous unequal treaties that severely tax her territorial integrity, her national sovereignty, her natural and patrimonial wealth. Aside from the port cities henceforth subjected to foreign powers, Hong Kong comes under the control of Great Britain in 1842; Indochina is taken over by France in 1874; Taiwan falls to Japan in 1895; and Manchuria is taken over by Russia the following year. And Shanghai becomes a concession that has its own government. Only the imperial organization prevents the Europeans from carving up China as they will Africa.

After two millenniums and several centuries, the Empire died out in 1912, a consequence of that succession of invasions, occupations, and dismemberments. The Republic was born out of this cascade of humiliations. But it is in turn assaulted from all sides. Russia extends its authority over Mongolia in 1916, at the very moment when Japan launches a major offensive with the aim of turning China into a Japanese protectorate. In 1931, Manchuria is conquered and, six years later, the occupation and the war waged by Japan harshly affect the State and the Chinese people.

The powers also intervene and with strength in China's internal conflicts, such as the oppositions between the forces of the regime of Sun Yat-Sen, those brought together by Chiang Kai-shek and those of Mao which are finally victorious. Then begins another chapter in the history of China and the world.

***

Spelled out on all the electronic sites, this demonstration has a precise target, "to get rid of the fallacious thesis of China's isolation and closing in on itself, encased in its dogmas, its rituals and values, isolated from the world and impenetrable. To get rid of the thesis of an aggressive, conquering and imperialistic China."

Wei Shu corrected in her own hand this interpretation of her country's history. She consults, deletes and enriches the contents of this message that strives to be definitive. She studies and re-studies the plan of action that aims to give the world a precise vision of the successive stages that have made China the way she has become.

***

Inaugurated in the autumn of 2033, Operation Qin Shi spreads out in all parts of the world. Under tight and effective control, "it puts wind into the wind," deploys the history of China during innumerable events held across the globe. China's joint ventures with her international partners are also recalled. Images of the Great Square are criss-crossed with the mythical places of the planet: The Christ of Rio, the Taj Mahal, Times Square, the Great Zimbabwe, the Island of Gorée, the Golden Pavilion in Kyoto, Red Square, the Pyramids of Egypt, the Mayan ones, the Machu Picchu, Angkor, the Great Mosque of Casablanca, Saint Peter's Square, the Eiffel Tower and many more still. The ideas of harmony and synthesis make up the common horizon of the greatest seduction offensive in history.

Spectacular celebrations are offered on all the world's screens and languages. Conversations are available with multilingual robots that specialize in Chinese rivers, jungles, primeval forests, cities and deserts; they specialize in games, too, that plunge you into everything Chinese and stun you through their novelty, their rhythm, their rational and emotional intimacy; there are games that invite you to confront algorithms with rare names that have stored up abundant reserves of intelligence, reflexes and humor.

The grand seduction is at work. The President repeats to all who want to listen: "Backing down is not possible. It would mean that China is humiliating China."

***

The *Shifu* congratulates Shu, later that night, for this souvenir of Suh Se-ok "discovered in New York." In the suite with old-fashioned decors, he related insistently this happy moment of their common life:

"Do you remember that Sunday full of light, on Fifth Avenue? You were wearing your dragonfly glasses and your large Moroccan purse. A rare moment of freedom, a rare moment for the two of us!

"Pizza with seafood, Chilean rosé, mango ice cream with raspberry coulis at a terrace decorated with flowers that "you loved amorously," according to your phrase that has become classic. In short, everything that you like. And right nearby, four or five doors further down, that large gallery like a little parlor, that elderly Korean woman and those wash drawings in Indian ink. You were silent. You, silent! Impossible, and yet! Filled with wonder and standing immobile for a long moment. Finally, you uttered: "This is what I have been trying to find for so long, a human representation that is nothing but kindness."

"The next day, I had gone to purchase those mesmerizing drawings. The elderly Korean lady had related to me the life of Suh Se-ok. I had thought for a moment that they had been lovers, real body and soul lovers. 'Yes, yes, Eun Jung, that was her name, answered me, I have been and still am in love with him, but he does not know it and he does not know me.' There you have the whole story. At the same time, I enhanced in your esteem, in your eyes, Madame President, my reputation as a cultural advisor and paid for your birthday gift.

"You know, before leaving her gallery, I had asked my new friend the meaning of her name, Eun Jung. 'The Kind one,' she had replied. The Kind one! The very word you had chosen to describe the drawings of Suh Se-ok. Your friend Lou Ye could make a wonderful film with these intersecting stories. And what a title: *Kindness*!"

CHAPTER XI

TOWARDS UNIVERSAL HARMONY

The President of the United States will leave Washington for the Popular Republic of China on Monday, April 30, 2040, at 16h30.

The President will be accompanied by the leaders of the House of Representatives and of the Senate as well as by eight members of the administration. The head of the American executive will remain in Shanghai until the following May 4, where he will attend the inauguration of the City of Harmony, the new seat of the United Nations.

Expected for weeks, this simple press release from the White House consecrates Chinese supremacy in world affairs on the diplomatic and political levels. It confirms its advantage in the vast debate concerning human development, this home ground for all the "western adventures" over the past five centuries, according to the expression of the Chinese President.

In its editorial of May 1st, the *Tribune de Genève* expresses the sentiment of many people:

Henceforth and for an indefinite period of time, the energy, direction and inspiration of history no longer depend predominantly on values engendered around the Mediterranean more than two millenniums ago. These values nourished the conceptual power, the individual and collective ethics as well as private and public law in the Occident, and they also strengthened its ability to impose them. The rest followed, from the advanced mastery of a material world to the architecture of its relationship to the other dimension and to the universal.

Another reserve of energies and directions, even more ancient, coming from Asia and the region around the Chinese Sea, is progressively sustaining values, conceptual power, individual and collective ethics, public and private law as well as the capacity to offer them as a legacy to the whole human family.

This reserve of energies and directions has been enriched, during this last half-century, through the incorporation of the values of liberalism into the Confucian ethic that filters them and guarantees them foundations that are renewed, indeed transformed.

The press release from the White House resembles a surrender, because the battle of the systems has been rapid, decisive and without concessions. In only a few decades, the third millennium has accorded Confucius the first, determining and sovereign place.

The President reads twice rather than once the American press release. Foreign Affairs have prepared a classic response, "warmly chilly," according to the President. "This is not in keeping with the event. You must forget this text and propose another for me. Put me in touch tomorrow with the American ambassador, this former number one of the NBA who sometimes takes shots at our net, and with accuracy."

***

"I am very touched by your thoughtfulness, Madame President.

--I am very grateful to your government for its rapid and positive reply, retorts Wei Shu. I would have wished to talk with you personally, but am away from the capital, at my summer residence, near the mountain of the Jade Dragon. You will have to come, one day. It is quite simply splendid, here.

In the vast enterprise that we are launching confidently, we will need the enduring support of America. I rejoice sincerely in the visit of your president. I will see him again with pleasure. Tell him on my behalf that he is welcome and that the members of his family, children and grandchildren, are my personal guests. They will fraternize with mine and I will organize an unforgettable visit to the Museum of the terra cotta army of the Emperor Qin Shi Huangdi. Convey to him that I will pull out all stops to ensure them a welcome which they will remember. And don't forget your promise to come one day, as you say, to play basketball with my grandson. You know, he is pestering me and is clamouring for you as a partner. I like this word partner between us. Here is an affair of state that you must resolve before it gets out of your hands."

***

The presidency, rather than Foreign Affairs, announces the visit of the head of the American government in engaging terms that surprise more than a few.

"The inauguration of the City of Harmony concerns all the nations of the world. Their representatives are all welcome. It pleases us to announce today the arrival of his Excellence the President of the United States of America. In addition to his wife and the members of his family, he will be accompanied by the leaders of the House of Representatives and of the Senate, as well as by eight members of the administration. We rejoice in their visit and will welcome them as partners of the utmost importance."

***

Dining with her principal collaborators, the President reacts forcefully to the words of one of them. He evokes ironically the visit of the head of "the former foremost world power, in decline today."

"Listen to me carefully, she had replied in her icy tone everyone knew, there will not be a parade of the victors as long as I will be here. I demand of each of you to make sure of it. Otherwise, I will restore the ancient torture of the beating, a torture from which one does not come out alive. There will be no parade of the victors for two reasons. Everything we undertake aims to change the narrative of international relations. So, lets tidy up. We have won too much up till now to begin to lose by alienating the meaning of what must come to pass.

"You know, when I wrote my report on the 21st century, I understood then that victory is often a curse that one inflicts upon oneself. I remember it constantly. I don't want any part of this curse, we don't want any part of it. Let the others set their traps and get their feet caught in them. They are used to it. After all, we are henceforth the trustees of what will happen to humanity, as far as one can see into the future.

"You know me; I am not going to back down by even one step when it comes to defending the national interests, but we must henceforth formulate them in a different way with those of the world's nations. You remember the words I said on the day of my investiture? I nurtured them for years. I have never stopped thinking about them and measuring their effects. 'All the nations of the Earth are only the diversified embodiment of the same humanity.' Such is the new archetype, the new promise according to which, henceforth, all are full-fledged subjects of history."

The President carefully avoids the references, the allusions and the typically French little phrases recalling the great conflict, "the great race," that pitted the United States against China since the beginning of the century. She has the choice of spokesmen. Personally, she holds fast to the position she learned from Lee Kuan Yew, the father of Singapore, on the occasion of his address before the Commission on China in the 21st century: *Advance without telling anyone and carefully measure the time necessary to travel through the space until the first rank, and then get to work.*

The President knows, and in very precise terms, how the path leading to this first rank has been heavy-going, full of military, political, financial, economic and "dialectic" risks, and that it went on until the second decade of the century. She also knows the number of victims which remained along the road. And then came Donald Trump, revealing what America had become, among other things, during the COVID-19 pandemic. Then the path appeared in a new light, China's advances increased as a result of America's rout, the shunting aside of its alliances and the disarray of it partners struck down by incoherent and sterile strategies. To win, according to Lee Kuan Yew, "is first and foremost to force oneself to prolong indefinitely the temporary amidst the realities of the world."

The commentators are divided. Rivers of words and judgments flow on the social networks.

"The universalist utopia born on the shores of the Mediterranean has been replaced by that of the great harmony bringer of universal peace arising from the former State of Lu twenty-six centuries ago. A new wisdom? A toxic ideology? A clever conceptual dressing covering up the worst scenario ending in domination? How can one decode such a proposal made possible by a dizzying acceleration of transformations that have taken place in the world?" asks *The Guardian*.

***

It is the holiday season in Beijing in this spring of 2040. The shifu keeps an eye open for problems. The dates have been decided, the services programed, the security, too. "Beloved, all we need is your signal to leave for your residence in the mountain of the Jade Dragon, with its gardens filled with peacocks, ducks and other ornaments."

The President prefers the Beidaihe complex in the municipality of Qinhuangdao, in Hebei province. Since the revolution, political leaders have flocked there for their vacations with their principal collaborators. It is three hundred kilometres from Beijing, a dream-like enclave bordered by the Bohai Sea, an almost perfect climate, tranquillity assured by police forces invisible but omnipresent. The place is historical. Mao used to pitch his tent there every year and, even as an old man, would swim like a young athlete. Those photos showing his head dominating the seas have gone around the globe. All his successors and aspiring successors have frequented Beidaihe. Some were successful in negotiating their promotion there; others drowned their illusions there.

As a child, the President would come there with her family, with her father who was then a member of the first circle of President Deng's advisers. She still likes the sherbets with the little red fruit flavor found on the main square, the corn cakes, the street food that floats out an agreeable and delicate aroma of shellfish; also, the softness of the seawater, even when a bit hot, and the possibility to observe birds which, she says, "make a pilgrimage there in the millions year after year."

People come to Beidaihe from everywhere to contemplate the orange birds in their mauve dresses, the striped ones which, they say, come from the heart of distant Africa, the great red beaks whose feet are almost invisible; the little phosphorescent ones that travel in a cloud and the invisible ones whose music, early in the morning, remind you that life, even when hidden, provides the sun with a daily procession.

These are many reasons for wanting to spend one's vacation in Beidaihe in the municipality of Qinhuangdao, in Hebei province...

"We won't go, said the *shifu*. You need rest, real rest, and you won't get it in Beidaihe. There will be visitors in the early morning, at noon, at 15 hours and in the evening, in addition to those near nighttime, audiences for all the careerists within a thousand kilometre radius, the long and mediocre dinners every evening, the scheduled encounters, the unscheduled ones and all the others. We won't go.

"Beloved, in a few days, you will be receiving the whole world for the inauguration of the City of Harmony. You must be at your best and be... how should I say it, Madame President, equal to your reputation. After all, you are the most powerful woman in the world; and also the most beautiful woman.

--Sir, you are dismissed, the President replies, dismissed for misuse of language, among other things.

--Then I will stay. So we will go to our villa in the mountain of the Jade Dragon nearby. You love it, and I, too, love that villa. You will be happy there, isolated, at peace. You will only have to endure the palace phantoms—Deng Xiaoping's—your humble servant, your cabinet scribes, the birds, fish and floating lotuses. I will be exemplary, attentive, affectionate, invisible or visible according to your desires. And also according to mine!

You have known this villa since your childhood. And, Madame President, you will not be bothered there, except by the phantoms of the monks who used to install there long ago their tents on the highest peaks, right next to the sun and amidst the mists it produces. Once the mists have cleared away, we will have a full view of the Jade Pagoda and Lake Kunming, the beauties of the place, aside from you obviously, which you shared with me when we came here for the first time. We were then almost clandestine lovers and we have remained lovers, as you tell me; clandestine, that's a bit complicated with you! So, you have made up your mind?"

***

The next morning, the presidential cortege crosses the city that is still asleep and enters the North-West Autoroute. All the avenues are blocked. Soldiers at attention form a guard of honor that goes on and on. Helicopters hover over the cortege that moves at top speed. The *shifu* takes a picture of the president asleep, draws nearer to her and offers her a resting place on his shoulder, He pinches himself, as though to say: "Here I am, a child of the Teheran suburbs, with Wei Shu for so many fulfilling and happy years now. And, I believe, many years to come and happy ones, too." He has been retelling for himself, and for more than the thousandth time, their first meeting.

When she entered the hall of the Security Council in New York for the first time, the high-ranking diplomats coming from all over the world rose and applauded her at length. She had not yet said anything, but she already dominated the minds and the place. A reputation "of the purest jade," an "imperial" carriage, a "symphonic" voice. The same question dominated all present: what in the world was this lady politician with an incomparable reputation doing in this galley ship of another era? Was she in exile from any ambition or orbiting towards all kinds of ambitions? A lever or a trap? And then, this assurance which I know now is fragile, but permanent.

"I thank you for this welcome that touches my heart. I will remember this moment. You know the word of a sage of our world: the mind can try to go further than the heart, it will never go as far."

I was subjugated and I still am.

As a project leader in the Secretariat General, I was entrusted with the responsibility of assisting the new ambassador of the Popular Republic of China at the United Nations in New York when she would arrive at the headquarters. I, Shahin Ahmadi, the son of an Iranian peasant, a forty-year-old bachelor, bald, historian of the Achaemenid Empire, researcher at the Secretariat General of the United Nations, here I was subjugated by a woman whom I saw for the first time. Subjugated, the word is weak. I have been living for years on the excitement that her presence, on that day, had touched off in me.

I knew everything about her, whatever one could know from biographies, notes, texts, photos and videos in the social medias, press articles and other sources. I knew everything, the known and the unknown, the luminous and the enigmatic! But, believe me, I knew nothing. Today, I know and I am in love with what I know.

How can I say it? Our first conversation has continued until today.

"Here I am in New York. You will help me to adapt and to never forget that there exist other worlds and other dreams, to quote my friend Arundhati Roy. Have you read The Secret of the Golden Flower?

-Yes, Madame, twice rather than once, and I will re-read it again. I am not sure I have understood everything well."

Then, she added: "You will help me adapt here and I will help you complete that reading."

There was in that sentence some kind of pact that I still understand. I believe I have lived up to her expectations. Every year, on the anniversary of this first meeting, I have delivered to her a bouquet composed of five-petal flowers from the plum tree, each one representing the five gods of happiness.

***

The least one can say is that the vacation at the residence at the mountain of the Jade Dragon is studious but happy. It is said that the gardens of the former imperial palace were designed in the 12th century and have changed little since then. One finds there the Xiangji temple, the Yufeng pagoda, the superb Jinxing and Furong palaces. Every day, the president and her *shifu* take an hour-long walk in this nature which, according to the Emperor Qianlong, "produces the most beautiful spring in the world."

We are alone, writes the President in her diary, *alone with the Chinese, Russian, American, Indian, Japanese and several other secret services. And in the evening, on the beautiful marble terrace, wrapped up in the same wool, we observe the stars and the satellites while wondering which ones are spying on us. They have all been like close friends to us since our time in New York.*

"Are we on vacation? The *shifu* asks imprudently.

-My dear, you know well, the business of the world never takes a vacation. It doesn't give in like I do to your whims," the President replies.

Wei Shu devotes a minimum of two hours, in the morning, to affairs of State, including the compulsory readings coming from the Palace, the secret notes from powers that are supposedly partners and from the others, the latter franker in their antagonism. At 18 hours, she rejoins her team for ninety minutes of discussions on so-called current affairs and future forecasting: the Party's and government's priorities, the international events to come and other "devourers of time." The atmosphere is relaxed. When on vacation, the President herself serves the tea, comments on the best vintages and the others, then asks about her counsellors' families, who are all vacationing in neighboring villas.

"You are telling me everything, except if you are thinking of divorce.

--That is not done during vacations.

--Then let's prolong the vacations by a century," the *shifu* interjects.

--Silence settles in, until the President says:

"Can someone, among you, tell me who this rhetor is?"

The crowd applauds.

For the time being, it is necessary to monitor the preparations for the encounter in Shanghai that will consecrate "the crazy inconvenience," according to Washington; "the new foundation for history," according to Beijing. Wei Shu is more concrete.

"It concerns the presence, in the most important city in the world, of the near-totality of nations to affix their signature on the new security and development pact to be shared by the whole human family." Che Se leads the discussions with "a vacation-like firmness." He intends to put a bit of sunlight in his phrases, also some *gusto*, like in Rome, or some *utsaha*, as in New Delhi.

The President insists that the contents of the opinions she will voice be enriched as concerns the following central problematic issues:

"How to shed light on the understanding and development of the world as a convergence of all heritages? How to think of nations, races, cultures and languages as the diversified embodiments of the same humanity?"

The *shifu* observed the President all day.

"You are really the granddaughter of He Zuonen and the daughter of Jiang Sicong. Like them, you keep refueling yourself. There, Madame President, I have said nothing except to remind you indirectly that we are on vacation. I have taken the time to think and I have reached the conclusion that your DNA would be grateful to you if you let it rock in your hammock or otherwise if you stopped thinking about anything—or about me—for a few days!"

By way of replying, the President shows him all the documentation on the school of Zhu Xi, "for reading and consultations during the vacation."

"I have made it my vacation project, she says.

--What, what, the school of Zhu Xi? Long live vacations!

--Yes, yes, the school of Zhu Xi. I return to it periodically. He who wishes to understand the yang and the yin of our civilization must impregnate himself with his teachings. It means deciding on the essential localization of things, in short, the main philosophical question. Are they all situated in eternal and absolute intangible principles, sources of truth and rectitude? Are they, on the contrary, in material forms that make up their natural abode?

--As for me, I have made my choice a long time ago, says the *shifu*. You are, Madame, this receptacle. Would you like a bit of African mango juice?

--My dear, give me one more moment to complete your philosophical culture, which is very deficient and very weak, just like so many other elements of your being. In all respects I am your Sherpa, and my determination is great. We will fill up these abysses.

-Yes, Madame, the *shifu* replies, in the most insipid tone possible. I am your gullible fool!

-Well then, listen to me carefully. I will speak slowly! The whole human destiny is in this choice. If the essential lies in intangible principles, then human destiny means leaving behind the appearances of nature and life in favor of the search and contemplation of these principles. Do you follow me?

--I will always follow you, and this mango juice? You haven't answered me."

Wei Shu holds her mother's last book.

"My dear, I will read you an excerpt from your mother-in-law's last book. She would have been shocked by your lack of culture, but she would have pulled you out of your inadequacies better than me. She would have loved you nonetheless! The first option dominated the Chinese way of thinking about the Universe, nature, existence until the 12th century. Residues of this belief are still present in several of our ritual activities, so full of meaning for us.

--And since then? the *shifu* asks.

--Here you are awakened, my dear, to the essential things. It was about time. I continue my reading: *This belief was overturned in the 13th century by the researchers of the school of* Zhu Xi, *who rehabilitated the essential theses of Confucius. Since then, and henceforth, the material forms are the ones that constitute the abode of fundamental principals. As a result, conducting experiments on nature and on Man's efforts at self improvement became necessities and essential practices.*

"*Social and personal ethics that prevailed in China for a thousand years, not only in China but also in Korea and Japan—the kind that Deng Xiaoping restores after the adventures and breakdowns with which we are familiar—are rooted in this doctrine to be explored through rationalism and pragmatism.* End of quote.

***

The discussion will resume at dinner, where different guests are present every night. The principal members of the civil cabinet have been invited this evening. After the usual chit-chat, the *shifu* engages in a monologue that ends with the following question: "What do you know and what do you think of the theses of the school of Zhu Xi?"

The surprise is obvious and generalized. Is the *shifu* really interested in that philosopher?

Che Se does not miss this opportunity to congratulate the *shifu* "on the rather recent loftiness of his intellectual, historical and philosophical interests." The President and her friends applaud lustily the words of the cabinet director who leaps in:

"My dear, there is a contemporary political incarnation of the theses of the school of Zhu Xi: Singapore. Yes, the Singaporean system. It concerns a body of convictions that are at the heart of the personal and social life, of the political and societal life of the people who inhabit Tumasik, the seaside city that is the former name of Singapore.

I am going to express myself simply to help you understand. The individual is made for society, and the latter cannot hoist itself beyond the levels of consciousness reached by the individuals. According to Lee Kuan Yew, the essence of the Confucian ethics is completely contained in the following statement: a society improves itself if the individuals who compose it also improve themselves. If an individual is good, then his family, his neighbors and his community will also be good, and communities of this nature will form an obliging nation. Hence the extreme importance given to education, to public spiritedness and work; Priority goes to collective rights, to responsibility inseparable from the enjoyment of rights."

All join the discussion, clarifying Che Se's statement. Thus, education is put forward as the instrument allowing for self-discovery. Some recall the significance of transmission, that arch of complementary, retroactive and prospective time spans; that linking up in a cohesive space of the past and past generations with generation to come.

The President speaks at length; she recalls "the recent origin of the *shifu's* intellectual, historical and philosophical questions."

"Better late than never. I allow myself to add to the statements I have heard the cult of ancestors and that of descendants, cults that combine and give a meaning to he who searches. In the first case, it consists in honoring the work of self-improvement and improvement of the world undertaken by the men and women of his past; in the second, it consists in offering the heritage received to the men and women of his future."

With her, politics is never far. After a long silence she adds:

"All this explains our fatigue in the face of the heavy insistence, the continuous harassment, the recurring condemnations coming from Westerners who are trustees of exclusive and imperial universal values; the condemnations of our fundamental values thought out and applied for thousands of years. The China of the 21ˢᵗ century is not the receptacle of a decanted West. She re-connects with the most enduring idea of herself, including that pact of integrity according to the teaching of Tseng-Tseu."

***

Later in the evening, in their apartments, she resumes the reading of her mother's book, and the *shifu* shows attentiveness and interest.

The school of Zhu Xi promotes a fixed method of proceeding in dealing with reality in order to recognize or inscribe in it the ensemble of feelings from the most general to the most intimate. It is at ease with the idea of bringing together fragments into the whole, with the idea that the whole will magnetize the elan of the body as well as the elan of the mind, individual experience and social practice. For the master, everyone exists because the others exist.

"Where the West atomizes, the East reassembles. Certainly, this whole does not have a metaphysical basis. It does not offer any salvation. Its aim is different. It consists in freeing oneself from the opaqueness of singular connections and in rising to a universal identity, so fully accomplished. So, from this unity flows singularity, that powerful paradox. On the highest threshold of human accomplishment, this empowerment leads, through successive stages, to the gates of completed experience and up till the inexpressible state experienced as knowledge without any goal. Once beyond those gates, one reaches the illumination of Buddhism, Nirvana.

"The void of beliefs is filled here with the fullness of experience; the absence of conceptual logic is filled with an unspeakable presence of the real, with a state of communion with the fundamental facts of existence.

"Whereas the West explains until it dislocates every ensemble, the East experiments until it reaches the all-inclusive body of the whole. From understanding this dualistic burden, one moves to seeing this limitless enrichment leading to liberation.

"The events in Asia reflect much more than the simple overtaking of one power by another, as it was the case at the beginning of the 20th century between Great Britain and the United States, those fragments of a same civilization. The rise of Asia marks the entrance into a new universal paradigm. It marks the rise of another conception of life, of relationships between individuals, of family ties, of relationships between the generations, of the meaning of work and responsibility, of the relationships between man and the world, the visible and the invisible. Finally, it boosts an ethical movement that models itself on daily rites and symbolic procedures, these components of individual harmony and common harmony.

"On this terrain, the West finds itself disarmed, its ethic is degraded and reduced to the formal order of law and human rights; its rituals and symbols are voided of their substance without any other substitute value except abstract rationality and narrow secularism. Mediation practices between generations have died out there; human loyalty is reduced to economic production; the tie to culture brought low down to the massive production of entertainment."

The western crisis and debacle had already been superbly summarized by Wei Shu when she was head of the Chinese diplomatic mission at the United Nations: "The West still exists, but there are no longer any Westerners."

CHAPTER XII

SHANGHAI 2040

THE CITY OF HARMONY DISPLAYS ITS SPLENDORS IN THE VERY HEART OF Shanghai, the capital of a province of more than four hundred million inhabitants, the financial, commercial and industrial heart of China and the world. For the President Wei Shu, this unique city illustrates "the pride of what we have accomplished over the past fifty years, one of the greatest success stories in human history."

On this first day of May 2040, Shanghai welcomes the heads of almost all the world's states. They have come to the Chinese metropolis for the inauguration of the new seat of the United Nations offered by Beijing to the international community, an offer as generous as it is non-negotiable.

***

Fifteen years earlier, in 2025, a first vote at the General Assembly of the United Nations had marked the official debut of the great public debate about the move of the glass palace from New York to Shanghai. Naturally, the proposal had suffered a defeat, but the movement it was generating, in New York and the rest of the world, had even then seemed irreversible. And it was, indeed, so.

China's diplomatic offensive had shown an intensity never before equalled during the contemporary period. One hundred percent of the heads of state had received in their capitals the President, Prime Minister or a member of the Chinese government accompanied by sizeable delegations. One hundred percent had been invited to Beijing.

Ten years and thousands of consultations later, the Assembly's decision had come, a majority and determined one. The countries of Asia, including India, Japan, Indonesia, Malaya, Vietnam, Korea, the Philippines; all the countries of Africa, with only five exceptions, the countries of the Gulf; the almost total number of the countries in Western, Central and Eastern Europe, including Russia, Germany, France and Italy; a strong majority of countries in Latin America and the Caribbean, including Brazil, Mexico and Columbia, had given their support to China and voted for the change.

The United States had suffered a terrible defeat, because their attempt to put together a "majority for freedom" could never be materialized. Presidential visits on three continents, marked by enticing alliance offers and considerable loans; international conferences announced then cancelled without explanations; threats of withdrawal from the United Nations on the very day when the seat of the Organization was to move from New York to Shanghai... All that had been notoriously insufficient. The defeat, a massive one, had been all the more painful for the United States because it had been largely interpreted as a referendum result that opposed the two powers. Washington thundered forth.

"The anger of weak people never lasts long," Wei Shu had declared at the time. The murderous phrase had gone around the globe several times.

***

In Shanghai, on this first day of May 2040, that arrow's full meaning can be felt when the usher announcing the entrance of the heads of state notifies, in a uniform tone in the Chinese language and the English language, and in that order, the arrival of His Excellence the President of the United States of America.

The latter is accompanied by three members of his delegation, a quota imposed on all the heads of state. The White House protocol demanded that no photo be taken of the person of the President and his delegation and that a discrete exit be arranged for him. This kind of understanding flourishes in the gardens of high-stakes politics, where are carefully counted the points acquired that eventually make it possible to obtain a useful dispensation.

The world medias insist on the mortifying nature of the American President's sojourn in Shanghai, ninety years after the inauguration of the United Nations headquarters, on January 9 1951 on the shore of the East River, in the Turtle Bay neighborhood, in Manhattan, New York. The very idea that this headquarters could not be in the United States was at the time unthinkable. There had been hesitation between Philadelphia, Boston and San Francisco, but the Rockefeller family had offered the American government the site that was finally chosen, and the architects Harrison, Niemeyer and Le Corbusier had picked up the challenge and launched the glass palace very high up, as a symbol of the longed-for transparency in international relations.

The City of Harmony, the new headquarters of the United Nations, rests on an immense stretch of smooth coral-colored water suffused with white light. By placing the City between earth and sky, the architects have reinforced the *Tien-hià*, that ancient Chinese belief according to which the world consists in what is under the sky far more than what is on Earth. In addition, they have given its full meaning to the name Shanghai, which signifies "the city on the sea." The initial plan was decided upon by a team of young Ethiopian architects that won an international competition. The plan was revised and enriched by the urbanist teams of the City and the University Jiao-tong of Shanghai.

Light is the unifying concept of this immense project which, inspired by an ancient local legend, must show the movement of the sky that leans over every evening to allow light to draw closer to mankind.

Made of buildings that espouse the stylized forms of the five continents, the City seems to float over a sea of light without any ties to matter; a pacified and pacifying sea. Its movements reflect fragments of galaxies that circulate in outer space and dissolve into it mysteriously. Two ginkgo trees more than a thousand years old and thirty metres high shoot up from the water and their images are reflected in it. They provide the framework for two bronze doors, copies patterned on the Doors of Celestial Purity which, since 1420, open onto the private domain of the Emperor in the Forbidden City. For millenniums now, Chinese medicine has been using the leaves and roots of these giant trees to fabricate concoctions which, they say, cure insanity. A columnist writes: "This choice needs no comment, in this place of all the debates to come, the salutary ones and all the others."

One reaches the City of Harmony through a long glass alleyway lined with bodhi trees, the exact replica of the western alleyway of the Palace of Peaceful Longevity in the Forbidden City. This alleyway was taken by the emperors to mark the exceptional nature of the day.

A vast cupola of blueish glass covers the five buildings representing the continents as well as the central building. Baptized the Hall of Lights, the latter houses the hall of the General Assembly and the circular succession of culture salons of the world that surround it. The salons open onto a sumptuous Zen garden where rest in a perfect order stones coming from the most celebrated places in the world: Axoum, Machu Picchu, Xi'an, Angkor, Athens, Fes, Madras, Rome, Jerusalem, Bagdad, Grand Zimbabwe, Mecca, Alexandria, Nara and so many others still. Drawn out in white sand, delicate and long furrows seem to blend into it and to have easily lodged themselves there just before the origin of all things.

***

That day, the President enacts all her personal and political loyalties. At the presidential residence in Shanghai, she has breakfast with two friends happy to see one another again, her father and her predecessor in the presidency of the Republic. Thus are again reunited the two Chinese students who were in the United States during the 1960s, and who are now the two grandfathers of her children. Afterwards, she makes a stop at the headquarters of the Assembly of Shanghai Province to greet the former presidents, prime ministers, members of the Central Committee and of the Party committees from the twenty-three provinces, as well as the former members of the Military Commission. Finally, moving from history that has already unfolded to history in the making, the President meets the representatives of the National Popular Assembly gathered in the vast vestibule of the Museum of Contemporary Art of the city. At every stage she takes up again essentially the same themes evoked since the morning: "The circumstances are meta-historical. They express the completion of a trajectory in China of about four thousand years and syntheses built up at different epochs of her history dealing with governance, justice and shared development."

At exactly noon, the President of the Popular Republic of China makes her entrance in the immense hall of the General Assembly. Radiant, in a white *qipao* adorned with her necklace of black pearls, Wei Shu enters the great hall called the Hall of Eternal Reconciliation.

157

She stands for a long moment on the threshold and contemplates the venue, which is magnificent, and in this venue, the assembly of all the political leaders of the planet brought together in the oldest country in the world.

***

I thought while this old country that is so modern was offering its reserves of philosophical and political discernment to the community of nations. At that precise moment, she writes in her diary, *I saw the long parade of our sages led by Confucius, the march of the highest political leaders of our history since the first Emperor Fuxi, also the faces of the historians who have kept the imprints of their exploits and, among them, my grandmother and my mother, then the great love of their intellectual life, Sima Quian. Then I saw the two women of my life in the village, as I saw them, when I was a little girl, wrapped in large red* han fu *that glowed in the night. I heard the voice of my grandmother joking in a low voice, between long silences, about the fact that the fire did not want to die out. "Perhaps, my mother remarked, it will never die out." This statement has been haunting me ever since, because the pendulum swinging between the ephemeral and the imperishable is so much at the heart of doubt in all things.*

The *shifu* gives the notebook back to Wei Shu.

"I knew it, I knew it. I saw you suddenly slowing down and slowing down even more. You then entered this world that no one knows, except you. These moments move me deeply, because it is impossible to guess if it is sadness or felicity that inhabits you at the time. I have seen you falter between these antipodes of the heart. You were sometimes in that state, at the Security Council in New York, when suddenly a convergence emerged from all the stagnation of international life. You told me one day: 'Jubilation melts in my heart, because these moments are rare and regression lies in wait for them like a famished jackal.'

***

A long ovation greets the President. She acknowledges it generously by using the *gong shou*, a traditional Chinese gesture, with palm over fist, then hands joined in the manner of Gandhi. She remains thus for a long moment, in front of this incomparable audience. Then she takes her seat, immobile, absorbed in herself.

"Dear friend, she will say to the *shifu* that evening, I was personally and psychologically savouring this memorable historical moment. All the world's nations brought together by China around an intention flowing from its history and its philosophy."

On the podium, she looks out at this unique assembly and opens the briefcase marked with the presidential seal placed in front of her at the moment when there appears on vast screens: *Welcome to the City of Harmony.*

She repeats this "Welcome to the City of Harmony" and continues:

"Welcome to Shanghai, welcome to China, welcome to Asia.

"Allow me to share in your name our common conviction with billions of people who see and will see the images of this historic moment. With their specificities, all the nations of the Earth embody the same humanity. Such is the certitude that unites us, the basis of our common responsibility, the foundation of our deliberations and the gauge of our decisions.

"A new era in the history of humanity begins today in this City of Harmony."

These words of welcome are taken up by the President in the principal languages of the world, Hindi, Arabic, English, Spanish, Russian, Swahili and French.

On the vast screens spread around the city and in Beijing, the words expressed in each of these languages encircle the blue planet like a kind and luminous crown. "With their specificities, all the nations of the Earth embody the same humanity." Half-doctrine, half-slogan, inclusive and accessible, this simple phrase will be taken up a thousand and one times to describe this exceptional day.

"This City of Harmony belongs to all the nations. Yesterday, during a brief symbolic ceremony, its legal property was transferred to their leaders.

"We are gathered here and we will gather here in the future to guarantee, as much in the historical sphere as in the digital sphere, our common security, the perennity of our planet and its social, environmental and economic development, those complementary sectors. Also, to guarantee respect for the linguistic and cultural diversity of humanity and to favor an exacting taking into account of each and everyone's responsibilities and rights. A new era in the history of humanity begins today in this City of Harmony.

"I salute the initiatives which, for a century and a half, have striven to bring together in the same organization the whole body of then sovereign nations. These initiatives were condemned in advance. Fortunately, ours distinguishes itself from them absolutely.

"For the first time, all the nations of the world have come together freely. In 1919 and in 1945, such was not the case as concerned the League of Nations and the Organization of the United Nations. One can say that at the origin of these gatherings, a near majority of the world's nations, enslaved and colonized at the time, found themselves excluded *de facto* from them.

"For the first time in the history of humanity, on this day, in the city of Shanghai, all the nations of the world have come together freely.

"Our meeting distinguishes itself also by the purposes that justify it. We have not assembled here as a result of incommensurable dramas, as in 1919 and in 1945; as a result of world wars launched from Europe towards the planet and which were the most murderous conflicts in history, with almost one hundred million deaths."

"It is not the horror of the barbarity that guides us this time, but rather the requirement to expel it from our humanity once and for all; then the necessity to offset the inhuman conditions in which an increasingly large number of our contemporaries are presently living. I will recall only two examples. I am thinking of the tens of millions of victims of grave climactic ordeals that are multiplying all over our planet; also, of the innumerable victims who suffer from our delays, in this digital era, in breathing life for seven billion users into an imperious and exhaustive juridical system that fixes firmly the responsibilities and rights of all. This lawless space is continuously expanding.

"I am taking advantage of your presence to propose two series of international conferences The first would be devoted to the unity of man and nature. It would meet, every year, for the next ten years, for the purpose of mastering the world-wide climate upheaval that is destroying in an accelerated manner our planetary space and is generating an ecological suffering that is reaching new summits everywhere. The second series, which would also take place annually for the next ten years, would have as its mission to lay the foundations of the juridical system for the digital era previously mentioned.

"Here we are assembled to assert and deploy a common will made up of the ensemble of individual ones to ensure that our demands for harmony fully materialize.

"We are going to build our common house on the formidable assets acquired during the last century. I will recall three of them among the large number.

"The rise to responsibility of almost one country out of two in the world, after centuries of domination, oppression and suffering, and its corollary, the liberation of almost two billion human beings who were enslaved. Secondly, the new distribution of the world's wealth and the henceforth largely shared ability to produce it in all parts of this earth. Since the beginning of the century, this transformation has radically changed international, scientific, technological, economic, financial and commercial relationships. Finally, another major given, the universal deployment of the digital era. For the first time in the history of humanity, a technological revolution has not occurred in one country or one region of the world. It is the shared experience in real time of the whole human family. Today, the Indian, African and Chinese communities of internauts total seven billion five hundred million Internet users. These categories did not exist one-half century ago.

"Now predominant, a new economy is born from this extraordinary doubling of our vital spaces, a new economy carried by human intelligence in conjunction with artificial intelligence, this fourth industrial revolution the incommensurable power of which is known to you. Our decisions will have to react to this body of reconfigurations, education will have to promote them, our institutions will have to respect them, and our policies will have to protect them. Together, we will make of this transition from the historical civilization to the digital civilization that is accelerating, our common success on the ethical, juridical and cultural levels.

"I say this solemnly, there will be no Asian or Chinese domination of the world. I repeat this, there will be no domination, either Chinese or Asian, over the affairs of the world.

"Let us take a common oath according to which, in extended time and deep space, we will work in such a way that the notion of closed frontiers will fade and that the notion of open frontiers will develop in all minds, so that they may take precedence over everything.

"Each nation will bring its own experience. China will emphasize hers which is almost four thousand years old. Its new synthesis has enabled her, during the last century, to draw closer to harmony by drawing out of poverty more than a billion of my fellow-citizens.

This thousand-year-old experience is shared with our Asian neighbors and partners, whose unity achieved and recently affirmed rests on vast common, material and immaterial transitions. This is the path to follow.

"The era of 'universal values' proclaimed by some and sustained by powerful systems of propaganda and oppression has exhausted its evil effects. Each one has come to our common table with the power of his heritage and the historical depth of his convictions. We need this diversity. It is neither superfluous, nor anecdotal nor optional. It is our framework. We must, then, pick up the challenge of uncovering the points of convergence.

"We are in the 21st century and not in the 19th, including all of you and China and Asia as well. Without complexes or triumphalism, we will occupy in it our place with references, attitudes and simple words fashioned over the millenniums.

"Our most ancient and most modern conviction concerns the central position of culture in human life and in the life of societies."

Here is fodder to exalt internauts, who dissect with gluttony Wei Shu's words. The clan of admirers have trouble containing the clan of detractors, whose "eyes have burst as a result of such an excess of mirages," according to the statement of "a frightened friend." As it unfolds, the speech piles up all the qualifying adjectives: indispensable, hypocritical, leaden, inspired, ideological, naïve, weak, inspiring, disquieting, predictable...

"What? Writes a Moroccan, the City of Harmony! The biggest hoax since the bird nest of the 2008 Olympic Games."

Certain people applaud "the thrashing that Europe is getting and the silence surrounding America."

Others celebrate "the new era that is breaking away from historical dominations."

A Brazilian is delighted that responsibilities and rights keep company with one another and says that he hopes the Chinese-style divorce will not break him too quickly.

A collective of dissident Asians "issues a warning against the seductive charm of that woman who is leading a world invasion of minds...".

"Ladies and gentlemen heads of State and of government, our common determination also aims to change the relationship with culture in order to restore its primacy. We are humanity because, over the long haul, generation after generation, in all societies and in all parts of the globe, human beings have created an abundance of languages, a multiplicity of narratives on an incalculable number of essential subjects, all connected to life, that of individuals, of communities, of the planet, and of the Universe.

"For each of these essential subjects, there exists an infinite plurality of perspectives, the visible ones and all the others, innumerable, that bear witness to the magnificence and richness of life and of the inexhaustible fecundity of the spirit. This plurality is the wealth we share in common. Like nature, it must be defended and safeguarded. The ignorance or the rejection of this evidence has plunged the planet, during an important part of the last millennium, into an unworthy and humiliating game for the majority of the nations of the world. If vengeance is excluded, amnesia would be disastrous.

"The time has come to proclaim and ensure the integral respect for cultures, this heart of nations, to rediscover the foundations for peace through this proclamation and common assurance.

"The collapse of the systems of cultural and scientific domination do not leave us without means and without projects. On the contrary, the virulent struggle and the widespread destruction that provoked it, that invisible war led by so many peoples, calls for a reconstruction on other foundations and other purposes. Let us celebrate today the end of a grotesque equation based on the belief that world culture flows from only one or several sources instead of being a great movement towards essential convergences. The vast domain of culture cannot be kept alive by mere market forces. That path is contrary to the harmony within the human family. It imposes uniformity where plurality must live. It dissolves all differences, denies and destroys them, thereby pulverizing the building materials for the unity and harmony of the human family. It has created during the modern and contemporary periods a generalized colonization of minds and peoples, an apparent globalization, but without roots or values.

"A new era begins here and today, in this City of Harmony. It will be marked particularly by the production of a new international public law, of which the first chapter will have to protect life, namely, the natural conditions of its emergence and its duration. This law will be nourished by our shared aspiration to replace an order of domination by an order of participation. This universal charter will recognize the unity of the human family, but also the mystery and reality of the multiple paths that man's genius has opened in all parts of the planet.

"A new era begins here and today, in this City of Harmony. It will light the way for the millennium that is beginning. In times to come, Shanghai 2040 will be celebrated."

The assembly rises and profusely applauds the granddaughter of He Zuonen and the child of Jiang Sicgong. She acknowledges this generously by using again the *gong shou*. She remains standing with her hands joined in front of this incomparable audience. Here is the world brought together in China, here is the intuition of President Deng Xiaoping transformed into a universal burst of energy.

***

Night falls slowly on Shanghai, which has become the keystone of a huge and essential venture drawing in all the nations of the world. In the library of the presidential residence, the family clan is reunited: the two grandfathers; the children and their spouses; the grandchildren; Ma, the only sister, the intimate, omnipresent and discreet friend all at once, a confidant and advisor, her husband Liang, president of China Railway which receives four billion travelers annually, and their children accompanied by their spouses and children; two uncles and three aunts; cousins male and female, then a good dozen close friends. Effervescence spurts up in the family around Shu's allocution, her assurance, her kindly and firm tone, and the contents of her speech. They also talk about the activities of the members of the clan, the trips, the studies, the health, the memories—especially the ones that recall He Zuonen, who would have been overjoyed by the accomplishment of her granddaughter for China and for the world.

In an adjoining salon, China's first team, as the civil cabinet is designated, is gathered around Che Se, "the other boss." He proposes a grand tour of the world: "It is early morning in Moscow, in Cairo, in Teheran, in Mumbai; it will soon be morning in Abuja and in Rome; Hanoi, London, Rio then Washington will follow. In truth, wherever one may be on this planet, the light of dawn will reveal our President as well as her Shanghai speech and her project for the nations of the world. It will also show the beauty of the City of Harmony and the hope aroused by this "beginning of a new era.""

***

It is almost midnight when the President returns to the residence and joins her guests. She offered a big dinner for the heads of State and governments, made the appropriate speech, took the formal customary photos and, in her limousine, finally "rolled herself up in a ball" near, very near, her *shifu*, who is holding her hand. He respects her silence. She doesn't say a word while they are crossing the new world capital at high speed. The *shifu* knows that his companion needs this respite after having deployed in one day an extraordinary outpouring of empathy towards the cultures, populations and nations of the world. She does not say anything. He does not say anything. Everything is in the live memory and the quality of an exceptional accomplishment which is their common task.

She enters the large salon of peace where all her kin are assembled, "her two families," she endlessly hugs her old father and ex-father-in-law, her sister and her children, her old aunts and cousins both male and female who remind her of her youth.

"Thank you for not demanding a long speech, she says. My very, very dears, I have come to bid you good night, like my mother would do when I was small. Ma will remember it. She would tuck us in, would read us beautiful stories, then would tuck us in again. I would give a thousand times a thousand gold coins for her to be with us on this day. It is she, not me, who should be applauded, she and her mother, and her mother's mother, and so on, these are all the women of our country who guarded preciously, protected and transmitted generously the ageless precepts pertaining to our relationships with others, with nearby communities, with the nation and the world. Official history accords them very little place. One must see their faces and kindly spirits in this woman who conceived today the architecture of international relations for the times to come. Jiang Sicong's face imprinted itself in me during this whole unprecedented day. I owe her everything that allowed me to speak to the world as I have done today.

"This is what I said this evening in my short speech during the state dinner. I put my official text aside and asked about their parents, their children and grandchildren. I wanted our guests to return to their countries with the feeling that our future deliberations would find their meaning in the development, well-being and happiness of human beings like your granddaughters and grandsons, your mother or grandfather, your husband, you sister or brother. Thank you for coming, I leave you, but not before I tuck all of you in, male and female.

***

It is late at night when Shu closes her diary, which she has just enriched with three or four pages of her most intimate thoughts. Her *shifu* is accustomed to these moments that are so special when the greatest silence reigns. But what is going to happen surprises and affects him deeply. Shu brings him her diary and hands it to him open at the last page. Then he reads what follows:

How can I conclude such a day that has seen the realization of the most ambitious and visionary political objective of our time? I have been thinking about it for days on end.

The whole world calls him 'the shifu.' I have never used this word to name the prince of Ispahan, my precious companion and the source of my joy. As usual, I have felt him by my side all through this unique day. I know that a surplus of energy and assurance has come to me from him since the first day when I saw and loved him. I would be happy if tomorrow, breaking with years of utmost discretion, our photo made the front page in the world medias.

The *shifu* looks intensely at this woman whom he shares with the entire world and embraces her.

"What an adventure, President! At our very first encounter, you had told me that there existed other worlds and other dreams than those that take hold of us when we live in New York for too long. Since then, I have remembered these words at every instant of our life together. A thousand times thank you! Tonight, the entire globe shares those worlds and dreams that you made me discover from the day I saw you for the first time. You and I have taken an oath of truth. So allow me to tell you tonight that there exist other worlds and other dreams than those which will take hold of us when we will have lived too long in Shanghai. Thus revolves the invisible destiny of the world. You, obviously, know it. Wei Shu, I love you."

SHORT CHRONOLOGY

- 1976: Death of Mao Tse-Tung.
- 1976: Return from the United States of Wei Mao, the father of Wei Shu, and marriage to Jiang Sicong, her mother.
- 1977: Birth of Wei Shu.
- 1997: Election of Wei Shu as the head of the Youth League of the Chinese Communist Party.
- 2004: Marriage of Wei Shu to Fang Jie.
- 2006: Drawing up and publication of the report *China in the 21st Century.*
- 2025: Wei Shu named Minister for Economic Planning and Development.
- 2026: Election of Fang Zheng, ex-father-in-law of Wei Shu, as President of the Popular Republic of China.
- 2027: Wei Shu elected as a member of the Central Committee of the Chinese Communist Party and named Head of the Chinese Mission at the United Nations, in New York.
- 2032: 22nd Congress of the Party; renewal of Wei Shu's mandate as a member of the Central Committee.
- 2032: Signing on February 6 in Beijing of the founding document for the Union of Asian Nations, the first panel of Operation Qin Shi, the big project of Wei Shu.
- 2034: Wei Shu member of the Permanent Committee and President of the Priorities Committee.
- 2035: China, foremost economic power in the world; speech by Wei Shu in Berlin.

- 2036: November 15, election of Wei Shu as President of the Popular Republic of China.

- 2037: Presidential visit by Wei Shu to the United Kingdom (England) and private visit to the United States (Harvard University), in Cambridge, in Massachusetts) on October 4.

- 2040: May 1, the transfer of the headquarters of the United Nations from New York to Shanghai and the inauguration of the City of Harmony.